Trail to Boot Hill

TRAIL TO BOOT HILL

James Wesley

AVALON BOOKS
THOMAS BOUREGY AND COMPANY, INC.
22 EAST 60TH STREET • NEW YORK 10022

PRINTED IN THE UNITED STATES OF AMERICA
BY HADDON CRAFTSMEN, SCRANTON, PENNSYLVANIA

Trail to Boot Hill

CHAPTER ONE

The gaunt figure of Abel Fargo loomed, in the setting sun, like a phantom rising out of the earth. The sun glinted off his bared, burnished brown head, and his lean fingers gripped the brim of his new Stetson like the claws of an eagle fingering its prey.

He hitched his horse to a shrub, then straightened his sagging shoulders and gulped back the bitterness in his throat. He had never cried before in his life, and the hot tears that glittered in his blue eyes added to the hate and fury that boiled in his heaving chest.

The Fargos should never have been buried here in this neglected Boot Hill, a stopover on the way to hell for thieves and killers. Abel stared at the many make-shift markers, decaying and awry, the last tribute to men who had led lives of shame, for the most part.

If the old man he had run across, who was digging around in the garbage dump on the outskirts of the town, had not explained why and how the Fargos had been buried there, Abel would never have found the three graves. The old man was garrulous and eager to display his knowledge.

"Was them Fargo folks friends of yours, young feller?" he had asked.

"You could call them that, good friends," Abel had replied, not ready to expose his true identity. Of his past he knew only what Kolarosa had told him.

"Well, them good friends o' yours got themselves vilified by most o' the townfolk, who wouldn't even let them be buried in the church graveyard. I didn't take no sides in the squabble. But Max Dugger blacked their names as liars and thieves. There weren't nobody in town to bend Dugger's will. He had formed a Committee for Community Tranquility, an' had hired guns to back him up. Tony Dugger, Max's son, with Fester Lomas and Cy Short, were the guns of Tranquility. They made Dugger's orders stick."

"That was some accusation Dugger made against the Fargos," Abel said. "What proof did he have that they were liars and thieves?"

"Dugger didn't need no proof. He hired the minister who took Fargo's place, so God was on his side. He hired the sheriff, so the law was on his side. People who objected were put outta business, an' nobody would hire a man who didn't have Dugger's blessing."

"You aren't painting Dugger in very bright colors, old-timer," Abel had said.

"Nothing bright about Dugger except his wife with her fancy duds. And his daughter, who's blonde as butter an' jest as soft," the old man had said. "What the town needs is a good shakin' up. I've seen them top dogs with their hired guns stifle a town before."

"Isn't there one person in town who has a good word to say about the Fargo family?" Abel had asked. When he had ridden to Silverado to dig into his forgotten past, he had not expected to find a town cowed and bullied by one man.

"Them who might have had a good word, ain't got much to say. I was there during the ruckus an' the fire, but I was a drifter in them days. There was a quiet rumor that the Fargo family had another lad, a youngster who escaped the fire, but no trace could be found of him. That rumor bothered Max Dugger. He offered a reward to anybody who could find the kid, said he wanted to adopt him an' bring him up righteous-like. I figured Dugger was afeared the kid knew something Max didn't want made public."

The oldster's recital had stirred vague memories in Abel's mind, but he could remember nothing before the day he had found himself in the Gypsy camp being treated kindly and civilly.

He had thanked the old man for his information and, tossing him a dollar, he had proceeded according to the old man's instructions. Now he found himself in the dismal, weed-grown, neglected confines of Boot Hill, a place that was avoided by all honest folk except those with inordinate curiosity.

The legends on the weathered boards or the sagging crosses had been erased by wind and rain as though to give the bones beneath them the anonymity they deserved. Suddenly Abel broke through the high weeds into a cleared space, where three mounds of earth lay neatly defined and decorated with wild flowers. The whitewashed headboards bore no names, but he instinctively knew he had found the graves he was looking for.

Abel Fargo stood there fighting back the hot tears that glittered in his eyes. The wild flowers were wilted and bedraggled, but they were there, proof that somebody still cared and shared his grief. He knelt by the graves, surprising himself with the unexpected prayer that came from his lips.

It was more than a prayer, it was a vow that Max Dugger would pay for his injustice. Whatever crimes his father or mother had committed, and Abel could think of none except perhaps being stubborn, they deserved a better fate than this.

It was only through time and the confession of the Gypsy woman who had taken care of him that Abel had learned his true identity. On her deathbed Kolarosa had told him that she had found him unconscious in the barranca near Silverado to which he had escaped after a fire. She had told him that he had been badly scarred by burns, and even now there were still faint traces of the scars on his torso and his legs.

She also said that she had found a metal tag around his neck that had proclaimed him to be ABEL FARGO from Silverado. He had lost his memory and she had made no effort to revive it, considering him a son sent to her by God. In the way of the Gypsies she had learned the truth of what had happened in Silverado, but had kept it from him. It was after he heard her confession that he had made inquiries of his own, but no memory of his youth came back to him.

Here he stood now, not at the end of the trail, but only at the beginning. A beginning spawned by hatred and grief, a beginning that he felt must end in vengeance. His youth was still a mystery peopled by specters. There had to be a key to unlock the secrets of his mind, but where could he find it?

When the sun had set and twilight was merging into dusk, Abel was still on his knees. So engrossed was he in his thoughts that he was unaware of the intruder who had appeared until a voice aroused him.

"What are you doing here?" a girl asked.

Abel, shocked by this sudden intrusion, rose unsteadily to his feet. He stared in disbelief at the slim young woman with the windblown dark hair and accusing blue eyes. Her defiant body was clad in Levi's and a flannel shirt.

"Who—who are *you?*" Abel gasped.

"What are *you* doing here?" the girl repeated.

"I reckon I'm here to visit the graves of some people who shouldn't have ended in this godforsaken place."

"Were they friends of yours?" she asked.

"You might say so. I reckon I'll ask you the same question. What are *you* doin' here?"

"Did Max Dugger send you to spy on me?" the girl demanded in an accusing voice.

"I reckon I don't know just what you mean, miss. Why should I spy on you?"

"I don't know if I should answer that. You look honest, cowboy, but no hireling of Dugger's is to be trusted."

"Wait a minute, miss. We're getting way off the

track here. I'm no hireling of Dugger's, and I have no love for the man. What cause have you to fear him?"

"Because I won't bend to his will, he doesn't trust me. He thinks I know the whereabouts of someone he fears. Someone I once thought I might meet here. That's why I sneak up here at night dressed in pants."

"If you think those duds disguise the fact that you're a girl, you're fooling only yourself," Abel said.

"Well, I'm really here mostly to change the flowers on these graves." She indicated the blossoms she held in her arms.

"Who was it you once expected to meet, miss?" Abel inquired.

"It doesn't matter anymore. I've decided he's too scared to come back, or maybe he's dead. Nobody knows for sure if or how he escaped the fire. His twin brother and his parents were so disfigured by the flames it was impossible to identify them. It was agreed, though, that only three people were definitely recovered from the ashes."

Abel felt a quickening of his pulse at her words. "Did you say *twin* brother?" he asked in a shaky voice.

"Yes, his twin brother, Emil. Even as kids, Emil and I were very close. I often dreamed of marrying him when I grew up," the girl said with a catch in her throat.

"What's your name, miss?"

"My name's Denise Curtis."

"How could you tell which twin you were in love with—even just puppy love? Weren't the twins identical?"

"In looks, yes, but not in the way they acted. Emil

was a happy-go-lucky boy ready for a fight or a frolic. I guess that's what attracted me to him. His brother was serious, more cautious and dependable. But sometimes they pretended to be each other. Nobody was sure which one escaped. Their mother did put name tags on them so they could prove who they were."

Abel measured his words. "Didn't the one who burned have his name tag on him?" he said cautiously.

"The heat of the fire melted the name tag. All that could be deciphered was the letter "L" at the end of the name. His name was Emil. I'm sure he was *my* twin. Emil was the one who would have fought to the end and died with his folks."

"You didn't have a very high opinion of Abel, did you, Denise?"

"How did you know his name? Were you friends of theirs?"

Abel glossed over his slip of the tongue. "I said I was a friend of theirs—sort of. I—I didn't think Abel was all that bad."

"I didn't say he was *bad*. I've grown up since those days. I realize now that Abel was the levelheaded one. Perhaps that's how he escaped the fire, by keeping his wits about him. What's your name, cowboy? You haven't told me that." Her deep blue eyes were steady on his face.

Abel said, "First I got to know if I can trust you."

"I can't prove that. I'll give you my word, if that's enough of a bond. But if you're connected in any way with Max Dugger, forget it."

Abel brushed back his burnished hair and replaced his hat. He looked away for a moment from her steady gaze. When he met her eyes his flat-paned face was a solemn mask. "I'm Abel Fargo," he said bluntly.

Denise stiffened and a bit of temper clouded her face. "I don't believe you. You've been pulling my leg all this time. Why? Are you a spy for Dugger?"

"I'm no spy for anybody, Denise," he assured her.

"Then why did you pretend ignorance of what went on here years ago? Surely you should be the one to remember, or are you ashamed to confess your desertion of the family?"

"You've got it all wrong," he said. "Learning what went on here has turned my blood to gall and my heart to stone. I don't even remember you, even though you're standing here in front of me. But I'd like to know you. You're a beautiful girl with sympathy and spirit. Maybe you can help me remember. In the name of heaven I hope so! You can't possibly know the hell of having half your life blotted out. I was told by the woman who raised me that maybe terror had made me forget some horrible incident and what happened before it. But now I've got to know the truth—why my family was executed. You say I had a twin brother. Look at me, Denise. Don't I resemble him a mite?"

She stared at him, frowning in her concentration. "How could I know what Emil might look like after six years? He was fourteen when I knew him. Now he'd be twenty. You do resemble him in some ways, but everybody resembles someone else."

"What color were his eyes—his hair?" Abel prodded her.

"His eyes were blue. His hair was a little lighter than yours."

"My eyes are blue. And my hair was once lighter. It got darker in the last few years. Tell me, if you knew Emil's twin well enough, do you remember any mark on him, a birthmark, or scar?"

"Well, we sometimes went swimming in the pond below Bennet's mill. I remember Abel had a scar on his lower chest from a wooden arrow Emil shot at him when we were playing Indians. It never healed properly."

Abel's eyes lit up. He had forgotten about the scar. It had almost disappeared. He opened his shirt down to his belt and exposed his chest.

"Good heaven, what happened to you?" she asked.

"What do you mean?"

"The—the hair on your chest is growing in splotches."

Abel had forgotten about the scars he had received in the fire. When the hair on his chest had appeared, it had failed to grow on the worst of the scars. He had accepted that as natural when Kolarosa had explained it.

"I—I'm sorry," he said, noticing her bewilderment. "The splotches were caused by the scars I got in the fire. But the scar from the arrow is still there. It's faded somewhat."

Her eyes were wide and disturbed. For a moment she just stared at his mottled chest, moisture clouding her gaze. "Were you really burned that bad?" she asked in a husky voice.

"According to Kolarosa, the Gypsy woman who cared for me and claimed me for her son, my back was worse than my chest. With her remedies she managed to heal the scars so they're barely visible. The deepest scar is in my brain. My loss of memory is one thing she couldn't heal. Or maybe she didn't try to help me remember."

"Why—why, Abel, if you are Abel, wouldn't she try to help you remember?"

"She had the idea that God had sent me to her because she could not have a son of her own. She wanted me to be her son. Why do you doubt that I'm Abel?"

"It all happened so long ago. It's hard to be sure of anything. Anyway, if you lost your memory, what brought you back here?"

"When Kolarosa knew she was going to die, she told me about the fire in Silverado, how it started all at once, like an explosion. She was a fortune-teller, like many Gypsy women, and she plied her trade in the town, keeping my rescue a secret. She heard rumors which she discounted because Max Dugger had few real friends. Some hinted that my folks had been shot or killed somehow before the house was burned. I don't know what to believe—I apparently wasn't killed before the fire. Kolarosa also told me how to get to Silverado."

"But—but Boot Hill—what brought you here?" Denise persisted.

"I met an old man searching the garbage dump back yonder. He said he had no part in the trouble, being a stranger in town at the time, but he knew about the burial of your *friends,* the Fargos. The way he told it, there wasn't one person who stood up for them. Why? Am I the son of a friendless man?"

She turned her eyes away. "I was too young to know what it was all about. The way it happened was a mystery to me. I knew the Fargos resented Max Dugger and his high-handed ways. Fargo owned land that straddled Apache Creek and Dugger wanted it. Fargo wouldn't sell. They wrangled about it for some time before the fire. You should know something about that. You knew everything that went on at the Circle-F. You might have run across something suspicious that Dugger still wants kept quiet. Think back, Abel. You were a quiet boy keeping your feelings to yourself. I guess that's why I finally favored Emil. Oh, I once liked you the most. But he was easier to understand."

Abel tortured his brain, but that blank wall would not be breached. He looked across the country below the hill, hoping for some landmark, a barranca, anything to jog his mind. There was nothing. If this staunch, beautiful girl could not budge his mind, what chance had a landmark to perform a miracle?

"Why don't you just talk on, Denise? Tell me everything you know. I can't believe my folks were liars and thieves. That's what Dugger called them, according to the old man at the garbage dump. There must have been some reason for Dugger's indictment, though."

"That depends on how you look at it, Abel. A man—perhaps paid by Dugger—accused Joshua Fargo of stealing from him. It was never proved against Joshua, and the man disappeared soon after the accusation."

"What do you mean—disappeared?"

"Just what I said—disappeared."

"You mean killed, so he couldn't be questioned?"

"I wouldn't go so far as to say that. But, remember, your father took over the preaching job at the church when we had no minister and Dugger resented his accusations against usurers and one thing and another. Dugger bought himself a minister after the fire just like he bought himself a sheriff. You might say he bought God and the devil just to keep them out of his hair. People were averse to causing trouble, and Dugger let the business owners carry on just so they paid their taxes and gave him a discount on his purchases."

"How are your folks making out?" Abel inquired, disturbed by what she had told him.

"Oh, Dugger gave me the teaching job at the school—that is, he made sure the school board voted for me. After all, I'm the sister of his daughter-in-law," she said in a defensive voice.

Abel, startled by her statement, asked, "What do you mean by that?"

"My older sister, Alice—you remember her?—she married Dugger's son, Tony."

CHAPTER TWO

Denise's blunt words startled Abel. He did not remember her older sister, Alice. Try as he would, he could not even remember Denise, who stood right before him.

He banged a fist against his forehead in a desperate attempt to jog something loose. The picture that he got from his conversation with Denise was more complicated and foreboding than he had expected.

Evidently Max Dugger had made Silverado *his* town, with nobody to dispute him. The Gypsy tribe Abel had lived with had gone to other towns subdued by bullies and crooks. So he knew what sort of man Dugger was.

Finally, he said stiffly, "So your sister married Dugger's son. Isn't that something! What side does that put *you* on, Denise?"

"On my own side. I never understood my sister. She was older than I. I don't speak to her now, since she married Tony. Tony married her because she was blonde, beautiful, and full of spunk. She twists him around her finger. She made him build her a big house on a hill, with smooth, sawed lumber on the outside and plaster on the inside, just like in St. Louis or Chicago."

"If you're not sure of who I am, aren't you taking a chance telling me all this, Denise?" Abel inquired.

"Life is full of chances, Abel. I'm the teacher at Dugger's sufferance, one of his chattels. Deborah Maxwell is another chattel, existing because Dugger sends the girls at the Palace to her for frocks and furbelows. If she displeased him, he'd scare the other women in town away. Lars Larson at the general store depends on Dugger's freight line for supplies." Denise spoke with suppressed fury.

"Does Dugger know you come up here every day?"

"I don't come up every day. Once a week sometimes. Other times not for a month or two. It depends on the flowering of the desert plants. Right now there are several. I try to slip out of town unnoticed."

"You mean Dugger has a reward out—or something like that—after all these years?"

"Something like that. There are still bounty hunters around eager for a wad of money, even if it means killing."

"Killing? Killing who, Denise?"

"Me, perhaps. Certainly you. He'll never rest easy as long as you're on the loose. Can you remember anything you could charge him with that would drive him to such lengths?"

Abel pondered, then shook his head in frustration. "I reckon not," he said disconsolately.

"Didn't the Gypsies know anything?"

"If they did, they kept it from me. Kolarosa claimed me as her son and disclosed nothing about my past. Not till the very end. She was afraid of losing me," Abel said.

"What *did* you learn, living with the Gypsies?" Denise asked.

"I learned how to draw a gun faster than light, shoot straight. I learned how to read people's faces to figure out their intentions before they act. A Gypsy fortune-teller uses her common sense. She reads other people's minds by concentrating on their actions, their expressions, and the telltale looks in their eyes. You can learn a lot about people that way."

"I don't understand, Abel. Do you mean you've become a fortune-teller?" Denise inquired.

"Not a practicing fortune-teller. I just try to read people's faces, like I said. That's all there is to Gypsy magic."

Denise said, "I see. And can your Gypsy magic put life into the bones that lie under these mounds of earth?"

He sobered. "No, but it can demand payment for the viciousness that put them there. I'm bewildered about my past. Already I've met two people who have opened the closed door of it just a crack. And all I see is ugliness and deception. Maybe you're my magic wand, my crystal ball, or whatever, to open the door further. Won't you help me?" There was pleading in his voice.

Dusk was deepening into darkness and the spirits of the souls buried about them were infesting the dank air. Abel could still see the straight, slim form of Denise imprinted against the sky. He moved closer to the white oval of her face, and her serious eyes stared at him.

"Do you want me to bring back the dead?" she asked. "Do you want me to open old wounds and put life back into grievances that are quietly slumbering?"

"I want you to help me reclaim my birthright. So long as viciousness and injustice are ignored, men like Dugger will bilk their neighbors. Somebody has to fight him. Maybe that's why I was born. Maybe that's why I was spared in the fire. And maybe that's even why I met you here."

"You could take your father's place, Abel. You have the makings of a preacher. Do you think you're a better fighter than him?"

"I don't know, Denise. Maybe you can help me find out."

"How can I do that?"

"For a starter, tell me everything that happened here before I was rescued by the Gypsies," he urged her.

She moved close and put a hand on his arm, her fingers pressing. "Are you sure you want to know that, Abel?"

"I've got to know, Denise. I'm living in a twilight zone peopled by vicious enemies who, according to your story, threaten to destroy me. Either I remain in this place of doubt, or fight my way back to reality. I must know the truth. That's the only way I'll be able to make Dugger pay for what happened to my family."

"Maybe you should just go away and start a whole new life somewhere else. Forget Dugger ever existed.

Wouldn't that be better than trying to work a miracle?"

"I don't believe in miracles, Denise. I was taught by Kolarosa that miracles are the result of chicanery, hard work, or delusion," Abel replied.

"Amen," Denise agreed. "Max Dugger is master of all three, and he has a hole card to back him up."

"Such as?"

"Guns—in the hands of men who live by them," Denise told him solemnly.

"There are stronger weapons than guns," Abel retorted. "Hate, for one."

"You're deluding yourself, Abel. Hate has a way of consuming the hater. Sometimes it can destroy your good judgment, make you fail."

"Who's preaching now?" Abel said. "Look, I'm going to get back at Dugger one way or another. And you have some information that could help me. If you won't tell me what you know, I'll find out elsewhere. But I'd certainly appreciate it if you told me what you know about Dugger and my family."

She sighed. "All right. I'll tell you what I know and what was told to me. I'll skip our childhood, when we grew up together and you had eyes for no one but Ella Davis, with her long blonde hair and her big innocent eyes. I wanted to scratch them out, but that wouldn't have changed the color of her hair. You were partial to blondes and I was a brunette."

"If I was partial to blondes, I must have gotten over it. There are no blonde Gypsies, not in our group, anyway."

"So you had to romance the brunettes?" she queried.

Abel shook his head. "No romance. The Gypsies

kept their daughters away from me, partly because I was an interloper, and partly because of my red hair."

He tried desperately to dredge up the memory of Ella Davis with her big eyes, but he could not. He then tried to fit the girl before him into the hazy patchwork of his youth, but even with her standing right there, he could not remember her. And why should he? He could not even recall his own family.

Denise intruded into his thoughts. "If I tell you what happened, will you promise not to become a killer and bait for bounty hunters?"

"I can't promise anything until I know more, Denise. I may be forced to kill, and I hope to heaven it won't be an innocent man."

"Who are you to judge the innocent from the guilty? Sometimes the line between evil and good is a very thin line. Anyway, Max Dugger and his son have a firm grip on the town."

"What about your sister? You said she married Dugger's son, Tony," Abel prodded.

Denise was silent for a moment. "Alice does what Tony tells her to do," she said in a dull voice. "I don't see much of her."

"Does she approve of what the Duggers are doing?"

"I haven't asked her. She was more or less engaged to another cowboy, but he was killed in a shootout in the Palace Bar. It was rumored that Tony hired the man who killed him."

"Alice married Tony after that?" Abel asked.

"Perhaps she's smart. Now she lives like a queen without the sweat and drudgery of a rancher's wife. She makes Tony's life miserable at times by flirting with other men. When she has him almost crazy, she butters him up again. I'm not sure how much he'll take. One day he'll kill another man over her."

"Maybe that's what she wants—to get Tony executed by the law." Abel was thoughtful. "But by what law, Dugger's law? You say Tony's suspected of having one cowboy killed in order to have Alice to himself. It's not likely he'll get justice in Silverado."

"Enough about Alice," Denise said. "She's made her own bed. Let her lie in it. As you can see, I've accepted you as Abel Fargo. And it's your own family you want to know about. Don't you remember anything about them?"

"No, Denise, I don't."

"Didn't your foster mother tell you anything? You said she told you—"

"She told me all she knew," Abel explained. "She knew nothing about my parents, or what went on in Silverado. She knew only that I'd escaped from some fire, some terror, and found refuge in the barranca. She told me my parents had died in a fire near the town of Silverado, Arizona. And so I came here. Then the old man in the town's trash dump told me what he knew. But I need to know more."

"You mean about Dugger?" Denise asked.

"Yes—if he's the one who caused the trouble and killed my folks," Abel retorted.

"Your folks were killed in the fire. Their remains were buried here on Dugger's orders," Denise reminded him.

"Were the bodies of my folks examined for wounds?" Abel inquired.

"There wasn't much use. They were badly burned. Dugger paid for the funeral. Very few people came to it. My family was there, except for Alice."

"Why were my people ostracized, Denise?"

"I thought we went through that. Dugger didn't like your father. Your father was a very contentious man, Abel. He believed in an eye for an eye and a tooth for a tooth. He was also too trustful. He borrowed from the bank on his IOU's, and old man Mathews never pressed him for payment. Then Mathews died in a fatal accident. No one knew how he had died. They just found him dead at his desk. Foul play was hinted at but never proved. There was no visible wound. No one in Silverado was capable of making an autopsy to search for poison. It was agreed that he strangled on a quid of tobacco. He usually chewed tobacco in private, but not in public. Then Dugger came to town saying he was the heir of Mathews, and he had papers to prove it. Anyhow, he called in all overextended loans, your father's among them."

"Is that when the trouble started?" Abel asked.

"Yes. Dugger brought in a federal marshal to dispossess the delinquents, not giving them a chance to redeem their notes by selling off part of their assets. When he tried to dispossess your father, he had a fight on his hands. To consolidate the holdings he had acquired, Dugger needed your father's Circle-F with the water flowing down Apache Creek. But your father fought the marshal. It was then the ranch house burned, killing your folks. Somehow you escaped. Can't you remember anything about that?"

"I can't remember that. My mind blocked it all out—

the fire, everything. All I know is, Dugger has to pay for his sins!"

Suddenly Denise stiffened. In the white moonlight her face twisted into a mask of fear.

"Abel, watch out!" she warned sharply.

Abel lurched to one side. He saw the glint of moonlight on the knife as it pierced his side. Gypsies were no strangers to knives. He had learned to use them and defend himself against them. This sneak attack in the dark had caught him off guard, though. Swiftly he caught the man's arm as he raised the knife for another thrust. With a deft twist he threw the attacker over his hip.

Sprawled on the ground, the man snarled:

"I've been followin' this gal up here many times. Dugger let her come here as bait for a man he's willing to pay for. You're not gettin' away from me now, mister!"

The man launched himself at Abel, knife ready to slash and tear. Abel had no knife, and to shoot his six-gun would attract attention in the town. He felt the warm blood trickling from the knife wound in his side. He threw up his arm to fend off his attacker.

The knife slashed through his coat sleeve and ripped the flesh of his arm. Then came another wound, in the chest. Unmindful of his wounds, Abel locked his arm around the man's throat and cut off his breath. Gasping and struggling, the man tried to drive the knife home for a fatal blow, but Abel's arm tightened until the man's gasping stopped and his flailing arm hung limp.

"Abel you've killed him! Killed him without a sound or a weapon!" Denise said.

"It was him or me, Denise. I'm not ready—ready—to—to . . ." The loss of blood took its toll and he collapsed to the ground.

CHAPTER THREE

Abel was vaguely aware of Denise's opening his shirt and trying to staunch the bleeding of his wounds. He felt a strange lethargy possess him, a lethargy he could not dispel.

I'm dying, he thought. I'm spilling my blood over the graves of my kin, my life soaking into the soil to join them.

He felt the bandages Denise had bound over his wounds and wondered where she had found the material. He tried to see her, but she was a hazy figure like the ghouls who peopled his memory. Now she would become one of them. Vaguely he heard her voice coming from a seemingly long distance.

"Abel? Abel? Can you hear me?"

He lacked the breath to speak, but he managed to nod his head. He realized she might be in danger. The man with the knife might not be dead.

"I'll help you get up, Abel. I've got to get you on your horse. We've got to get out of here," she whispered as though his attacker might hear.

Denise moved his horse beside him and he felt her tugging at his shoulders. With the last dregs of his strength, he managed to come to a sitting position.

"Take hold of the stirrup and pull yourself up," she ordered him.

Some spurt of strength lifted him to his unsteady feet.

"Take hold of the saddle. I'll boost you into the seat."

Like a little boy he followed her instructions. And he vaguely felt the rope she used to tie him to his horse. Then he blacked out.

Sometime later he found himself lying in a bunk in a cabin, with the first shades of dawn coming through a grimy, unwashed window. For a long moment he lay still, unable to comprehend the situation. The events of the night before haunted him like a dream.

Then Abel realized the girl had to be real; the man he had strangled had to be real. But how had he come to be here in this cabin? He turned his head and inspected his surroundings. There was a cast-iron stove and some cupboards with barred doors to discourage rats. There was a table holding a candle half-eaten away by rats. There was a bench holding a wash basin and a water bucket.

His throat was dry and he had a deep thirst. His shirt

was gone, also his Levi's and boots. He had on only his long underpants. He rose unsteadily from the bunk and took two steps toward the water bucket, feeling feverish. Then Abel's knees buckled. He fell backward hitting his head against the bunk. Once more, blackness enveloped him.

Abel came to in an ominous world. Strange thoughts bedeviled him, thoughts of his youth, thoughts of quarrels and confrontations and shootouts. For a moment he lay puzzled, and then the truth dawned on him. The blow on his head when he had hit the bunk had unlocked his mind! This was a miracle he could not deny!

Denise's face floated above him, and her concerned voice penetrated his fogged mind. At first he couldn't make out her words. He knew only that he was free at last, free in a jungle of memories that taunted him.

"I'm sorry I had to leave you, Abel, but I had to go back and see about the man you strangled," she said contritely.

Her words were a jumble of sound to him, invading the drama infesting his awakened memory. The vision of his folks stood forth in stark reality: his father, stern and unyielding, his gaunt, rigid body defying aggression. His mother—her poignant face with its brown eyes tortured by the fear of evil—adamant in her loyalty to her husband. His brother, Emil, a young boy like a mirror reflection of himself.

Abel remembered the standoff at the ranch house, with guns blazing. Then he remembered the agony of the fire, started in the dead of night. He remembered climbing through the attic window with his clothing aflame. The last thing he remembered was running into the dark. Choked and nauseated by the terrible memories, he felt tears come to his eyes.

"Abel—Abel, what's the matter? What happened to you?" Denise asked.

"I—I tried to reach the water bucket to get a drink. And I fell and knocked my head against the bunk. Then I blacked out. When I came to, I remembered my past, my folks, the fight at the ranch, and the last thing I remembered was running into the darkness, hurting with pain."

"Oh, Abel, I'm sorry I left you alone," she said.

"No, don't be sorry, Denise. It was a blessing in disguise. Horrible as the truth is, I had to face it sometime. Why not now, with you to help me fill in the blank spaces? Now I know what drew me back here. And I'm twice as eager to get revenge."

"It's all over, Abel. It's been over for a long time. If you try to get even for the old wrongs, you might be killed. You're the only surviving member of the family. You can have sons to carry on the Fargo name. Maybe that's more important than getting revenge."

"I'd have sons to learn the truth, how their father had been too scared to see that justice was done. No, Denise, I want no sons of mine to think I'm a coward."

"You're preaching again, but I see your point. Do you remember what happened last night?"

"Of course, up to the time you got me on the horse. I don't remember getting into the cabin. How did you manage that?"

"There is more strength in a human body than people know of. I slid you off on my back and lugged you inside," she said with a touch of pride.

"What is this place? Where are we?"

"Don't you recognize it, Abel?"

He gave the place a closer inspection. It was vaguely familiar. Then he noticed the brand burned into the door. It was almost oblitered. The truth dawned on him and he shook his head.

"I don't believe it! This is a Circle-F line shack that belonged to my father," he said slowly.

"When we were kids, you, Emil, and I spent a night here when we were caught in a cloudburst," she said.

"I remember!" he said, his eyes lighting up with astonishment. "I actually remember! Our folks thought we were drowned for sure." Then his face grew serious. "But to get back to the present, what exactly did you do when you left me?"

"I went back to drag the man you strangled into the chaparral out of sight. I didn't know what else to do," she explained.

Abel forced the next question. "Was—was he dead?"

"I don't know whether he was dead or not."

"What does that mean?"

"He was gone—disappeared."

"Then I didn't kill him!" Abel exclaimed.

"He might have had a partner out in the chaparral who took his body away."

Abel was silent for a moment. He knew the repercussions that could come if the man were still alive.

"Did you see any sign of hoofprints?"

She shook her head. "He evidently walked to Boot Hill from town. It isn't far. I always walk. It's easier to slip up there unnoticed."

"You know what this means?"

"Yes," she answered. "It means Dugger might be prepared for your coming."

"I had hoped to slip into town under a false name and have a look around," he said. "I might still do that."

"It wouldn't work, Abel. Every stranger in town will be stopped and scrutinized. Now that you've got your memory back, can you recall anything you might know that would convict Dugger?"

He felt a wave of weakness returning. "Are—are my bandages still holding back the bleeding?"

"Well enough. The fall didn't disturb them. I brought the canteen in from your saddle. The water in the bucket isn't fit to drink. Here, let me hold your head."

She put a hand under his head and raised it so that he could drink from the canteen. He choked on the cool water, but he kept it down. He lay back, staring at the cobwebs festooning the roof boards. More details of his past slowly emerged from his unblocked memory.

He tried to think of anything that might link Dugger to the fire, but the memory of the flames was shrouded in a haze of smoke. He shuddered as the terror and pain of his escape from the house assailed him with stark realism. How could he, when he had leaped from the attic window and raced across the uneven ground with his clothes burning, have remembered any clue to link Dugger with the fire?

"All I can remember, Denise, is a blind, agonizing terror. My mind must have deserted me before I reached the barranca where Kolarosa found me. The water in the bottom of the barranca must have extinguished the flames before I was totally burned. As I told you, Kolarosa nursed me back to life, but she failed to revive my lost memory. There are still things that aren't clear."

"Give it time, Abel. The most terrible things in your memory might need extra time before they emerge. In the meanwhile we've got to get you to a place where you can be cared for properly. This line shack hasn't been used for years. The water is brackish and what food was left here for chance travelers is moldy and unfit for rats," Denise told him.

"It's near full daylight, Denise. If we travel, we'll be spotted. If you go back alone, you'll be in danger. Because if the man I strangled is still alive, your part in the affair will be known, even if he never got a good look at me in the dark. You're dead tired, and without much sleep. Lay low here today and tonight we can find another hideout. There should be some biscuits and jerky in my saddlebags. They'll keep us for today."

"Here," she said, surrendering his gun, which she had taken with her for protection when she had gone to dispose of the strangled man. "I could do with some more sleep."

Abel, himself fully awake after his period of unconsciousness, watched over her as she fell asleep the moment she closed her eyes. She looked so small and helpless lying there, in the cabin's second bunk, her young face composed and her chest rising and falling with each breath. She was a disturbing figure from his past, barely recognizable yet so poignantly concerned for him.

Her allegiance to the memory of his family and her avowed opposition to Max Dugger made her a friend he could depend on. But he had no intention of placing her in further danger.

He needed allies, that was for sure, but not pretty young girls whose trust and allegiance were based upon half-forgotten childhood recollections. Perhaps she might find him some confederates secretly sympathetic to the Fargos, men who might welcome a leader who would dare to face Dugger and expose him. Still, they'd all been afraid to fight Dugger before. Would they be willing to do so now?

Abel's returning memory aroused a new restlessness in him, an eagerness to get on with his fight to down Dugger from his high horse. His fever seemed to be gone. There was so much he needed to know and so little to go on. He vaguely remembered Dugger as a newcomer to Silverado, and knew that his father did not trust him, but he was never sure of the reasons.

He had been too young to understand legal complications. He only remembered that his father was an uncompromising man often involved in disputes over religious doctrine, condemned by those who resented his rigid viewpoint. There were others who respected him and agreed with his thunderous sermons, but they were not the kind of people likely to fight Dugger. Abel was not just looking for virtuous men; he was looking for resentful men, men who had lost part of their lives because of Dugger. Men with a grudge in their craw, who wanted to dislodge that grudge without getting involved with the law. Maybe even hired gunmen.

He recalled old rumors that men were being cheated by false witnesses and forged papers. Some of those men must still be near Silverado, hoping for the day when Dugger would be exposed and they could realize their claims against him.

After several hours had passed, Abel finished the last of the water in the canteen. Hoping to replenish the supply, he went in search of the spring he remembered being near the line shack. Dodging from juniper to juniper and crawling through the chaparral, he reached the spring, which was choked with needles from the nearby pinon tree.

He scooped out the needles and clawed away some of the dirt that had slid into the basin of the spring. With the eruption of clear, cool water free of debris, he filled the canteen and slaked his thirst. He felt hot and his head throbbed dully. Was infection setting into his wounds? He had the sickening thought that he might die before his mission was begun.

Returning to the shack, Abel found Denise awake and bright with renewed energy. But the smile with which she greeted him faded, to be replaced by a look of concern.

"What's the matter, Abel? You look flushed. How do you feel?" she asked apprehensively.

"I—I don't know," he stammered. "I—I think the fever is returning."

"Take off your shirt and lie down," she ordered.

"What can you do, Denise? Kolarosa made special poultices for me. That's how she—she cured my burns," he informed her.

"We have no time for poultices, Abel."

"Can't you get a doctor?" he asked, gritting his teeth against the mounting pain.

"That would be too late. You could be dead before he got here."

Abel took off his shirt. The smell of pus from his chest wound was strong. He watched Denise's small hands unwind the bandages.

"What can you do, Denise? You have nothing to work with," he lamented.

"I have a knife," she said. "I can lance the wound with that."

"What knife? I had no knife," he insisted.

"I found the knife that stabbed you on Boot Hill," she explained. "Got any whiskey in your saddlebags?"

He nodded.

Using the whiskey to dull the pain and as an antiseptic, Denise lanced Abel's wound. Then he lost consciousness again.

"How are we feeling now?" Denise's cheery voice was the first thing he heard when he returned to consciousness.

He looked up into her blue eyes that were glassy with unshed tears, belying the cheerful tone of her voice.

"Don't worry," he said. "I'll live."

"I guess you will. That Gypsy whiskey would kill any infection."

"It isn't Gypsy whiskey. I bought it in Bisbee," he said.

"What were you doing in Bisbee, and where did you

get the money to throw away on booze?" she demanded.

"I had business in Bisbee. It's a long story."

"Keep your business to yourself if you want. How do you feel?"

"Thanks to you, Denise, I feel better. What kind of a girl are you, anyway? You're grieving over the fate of my folks. You managed to get me to this line shack. And you saved me a second time by lancing my wound."

"I'm a woman, Abel. Women have strength when they need it."

Abel studied her. It was inconceivable that the girl he remembered in pigtails and freckles could have developed into such a person. For a moment he was jealous of Emil, who had won her favor.

"Denise, I'll never be able to repay you," he said solemnly.

"You can start repaying me by getting back enough strength to be moved from this line shack. Any wandering range rider might run across our tracks, or see your horse and stop in for a look-see. As soon as it's dusk, we're getting out of here."

"Where will we go?"

"To my home, that's the safest place. Nobody will look for you there."

"You could be seen and followed," he warned her.

"I know of a way to get there unnoticed," she said.

"But if the man who attacked me is still alive, he will have reported to Dugger about our meeting at Boot Hill."

"I don't think so, Abel. Dugger hates bunglers. Besides, the man can't be sure who you were. If he had killed you, he could have dragged you in for identification. And we're not sure that he's still alive."

"If he's not alive, then he has a friend who dragged him away," Abel reminded her.

"We're wasting time here making wild guesses. The sun has almost set. We'd better get ready to move," she told him.

"What about your folks?" he inquired pointedly. "Your sister is married to Tony Dugger. You're teaching school at Dugger's orders. What about your mother, your father?"

"My mother hides her resentment against Max Dugger, for Alice is still my mother's daughter. Her marriage didn't change that. My mother goes up to Alice's new house and sometimes stays there for days. Sometimes just for hours. My father has no love for the Duggers, but he's powerless to oppose them. He would welcome a chance to see Dugger brought down. Don't deny him that chance, Abel Fargo."

CHAPTER FOUR

Denise, walking ahead, led Abel's horse on a round-about trail that wound through the bottom of an arroyo, which shielded their presence from the town. Abel swayed weakly in the saddle with his hands secured to the horn.

The Curtis ranch was on the edge of town, a modest spread that provided only part of their livelihood. The balance was provided by Chris Curtis's blacksmith shop, which he ran in the town with the help of Rico Santos, a brawny Mexican. The moon was up by the time they reached the ranch.

Abel was too exhausted from his loss of blood and his infection to recognize any of his surroundings. He was half conscious of the horse climbing out of the arroyo and passing the corrals on the way to the house.

He heard Denise's voice call out:

"Pa, come out here. I need help!"

He was conscious of hands fumbling with the rope that secured him to the saddle horn. Then brawny arms were lifting him from the saddle and carrying him into the house. Soon he lay exhausted on a comfortable bed. He heard the man's voice talking.

"Go to the kitchen and fetch me some hot water and some fresh towels. I'll clean him up and get him into some of my underwear. After you bring the water, you can fix something to eat. There'll be time, Denise, to explain where you found the maverick and how he come to be in this bedraggled condition."

"I can fix him up, Pa. I'm not squeamish," Denise insisted.

"It ain't no job for a girl. We need Doc Haige to give us hand."

"No doctor, Pa, not yet. I'll explain why later. Do you recognize him, Pa?"

"Don't reckon I do. He might look better when he's cleaned up. Get goin', gal. I ain't sure he's alive."

Abel heard the conversation but lacked the energy to join in. There was too much to explain.

For the moment he lay there while Chris Curtis undressed him and cleaned him up. By the time the big man had bathed his face and raked back his hair, Abel felt enough strength returning to let him speak.

"I'm sorry I've become a problem for you, Mr. Curtis. I had no idea I'd be forced into this predicament. If not for your daughter, I would have bled to death on the graves of my parents."

The man's face looking down on him became clearer now, the iron-gray hair, the strong jaw, and the piercing eyes. The face was vaguely familiar.

"What do you mean, son, *the graves of your parents?"*

Abel took a deep breath. "Just what I said, sir. You wouldn't recognize me, I've grown up. My father was Joshua Fargo."

It was Chris Curtis's turn to take a deep breath. "Am I hearin' you right? There ain't no Fargos left alive. They was every one killed an' burned in the fire."

Denise came in and looked at Abel in her father's clean underwear, his wounds freshly bandaged.

"I heard what you said, Pa. They weren't all burned in the fire. Only enough charred remains were uncovered to definitely account for three victims: Joshua, Emma, and one of the twin sons."

Chris stared at her, his stern eyes half-closed. "What're you tryin' to tell me, Denny? You ain't surmisin' that this is the other twin, are you?"

Abel spoke for himself. "I am Abel Fargo. I know it's hard to believe after all these years."

"If that be so, why did you wait so long to come back?" Chris asked.

"He couldn't come back, Pa," Denise said defensively.

"Why not?"

"I was picked up by Gypsies, and my mind was a blank. Kolarosa, my Gypsy mother, told me some things on her deathbed. She told me who I was and how she had found me in a barranca burned and out of my head."

"Don't tire yourself, Abel," Denise said. "I'll explain it all to Father."

She told the story just as she had learned it from Abel's lips. She told her father about the meeting on Boot Hill, about the strangling of Abel's attacker, and about everything else.

"Dugger's reward for finding Abel still stands, Pa. But I'm sure he never wanted to raise Abel as a son. He wants him dead."

"Why?" Chris asked.

"Because Abel probably knows something that could destroy Dugger. Abel got his memory back when he struck his head on the bunk, but details are still missing. Another thing, the man Abel strangled wasn't at the graves when I went back to hide him in the brush. He could still be alive, or he had a partner who took his body away."

Chris, looming big in the lamplight, went over to the dresser, picked up his pipe, and tamped it full of tobacco. He got it going and he was silent for a moment, then returned to the bed. His mind was evidently mulling over all that he had heard. He removed the pipe from his thin lips.

"This is a fearsome thing you tell me, Denny. The old sores are healed over," he said gravely.

Denise disputed him.

"But they've not completely healed, Pa. They're still festering underneath."

"Mebbe so. From what you tell me, Abel's come back to prick them sores open. What's he gonna do once he opens 'em?"

"I aim to learn the truth, sir," Abel said.

"The truth could make you dead—stone dead. You can't fight Dugger with accusations. He owns the sheriff. He owns the church. He's got a cavvy of gunnies backin' him up. It takes more'n guts to fight back at Dugger. It takes money, m-o-n-e-y!"

"That's no problem, sir."

"What do you mean, son? I ain't never heard of a rich Gypsy."

"I told Denise that I'd been in Bisbee, but I didn't get a chance to explain why. My Gypsy mother was a fortune-teller. She told fortunes in all the mining camps. There was a silver mine near Bisbee owned by a man who had more faith than cash. He paid the men who worked for him half in cash and half in mining stock. The men took the money and traded off the stock for what they could get, considering it worthless.

"Kolarosa, with a Gypsy's intuition, took that stock for telling fortunes, lots of it because it was considered worthless. When she died, she turned the stock over to me. I went to Bisbee and discovered that the mine I held stock in had hit a bonanza in silver.

"There were uncollected dividends piled up in the bank in Kolarosa's account. She had signed the stock certificates over to me. So I found myself well-off, with the stock selling for ten dollars a share. No man who stands with me is going to lose money, with a bonus if things pan out the way I hope."

Chris Curtis took a drag on his pipe and emitted a cloud of smoke.

When Denise accused him of fogging the air, he retorted, "It ain't half as foggy as my mind. I'm asked to take this hombre on faith. I'll admit that mebbe he could be a Fargo, but whether he's Abel or Emil, I ain't sure."

"What difference does that make, Pa? He's a Fargo, and they were destroyed by Max Dugger—killed and cremated," Denise insisted.

"There weren't no proof of that, Denny," Chris objected. "Nobody came forward who actually seen them killed. There was just talk. There were no proof marks on the bodies that they were dead before the fire."

"The bodies were too charred to really be examined," Denise said. "Dugger had them degraded and accused of stealing, sworn to by a paid witness who disappeared after the accusation. When Abel's memory clears, he might remember something that could link Dugger to the killings and the fire."

"Wait a minute, Denny. You bring in a man who's half dead and tell me a tall story I'm supposed to swallow without question. You say this man—call him Abel if you want—escaped from a burnin' house, was found in a barranca half dead by a Gypsy who raised him an' gave him a fortune so he could come back here an' stir up trouble nobody wants. And first he lost his memory, and then it came right back. I'm supposed to believe that?"

"I know you didn't side with Joshua Fargo on his preachings of hellfire and demons, Pa, but you never faulted him when it came to honesty and neighborliness. Well, you can help Abel now. Believe him, trust him. Most of the ranchers and fiddle-footed cowboys come to your shop to have their horses shod. You can nose around and pick those who have a grudge against Dugger."

"There ain't nobody who don't have a grudge agin Dugger. There ain't many who ain't indebted to him, justly or unjustly. And there ain't any who'll invite his displeasure. Your mother right now is up at Alice's big house. She means to go there a lot more from now on. Alice's baby is expected any day now. Dugger ain't bothered me in my ranch or my business because me an' him is goin' to both be grandfathers when the kid is born."

"I hope Alice is happy," Denise said with a touch of rancor. "She'll have a little Dugger to tie her to the king of the town."

"Hold your spite, gal," Chris reprimanded her. "Alice ain't as happy as you imply. She married Tony Dugger partly to keep us from bein' kicked off Apache Creek."

"I'm sorry if I faulted her, Pa. If she sacrificed love for convenience, I'm sorry for her," Denise said.

"Mebbe she's practical, Denny. Mebbe she figures it's smart to grab onto the material things an' learn to love her man in time."

"Is that why she devils Tony with her flirtations?"

"She don't devil him so much no more," Chris informed her. "Not as much as before."

"Is that so? He's been drinking more than average lately," Denise countered.

"How in blazes did we get sidetracked onto Alice's problems? We was discussin' Abel here. Mebbe I'll help him. I ain't sure what your ma will say to all this. She wouldn't want to make trouble for Alice."

"Forget Alice, Pa. Have you got any idea, any men you've dealt with who might help Abel?"

Chris was thoughtful for a moment. "There's three strange hombres who moved into town who is courtin' Dugger's displeasure. They ain't buckin' him directly, but they's ingratiatin' themselves to the citizens by donatin' money to the school board, an' the church. What their games is I ain't got no idea. I ain't run across anybody like them before. They's free with their money. One of 'em lives in town, goes to church, an' is sparkin' Dugger's daughter, Irma."

"What are their names?" Abel asked. "I've run across all kinds along the border. A Gypsy camp is always on the move. Once I was called out by two men dressed like sodbusters. They turned out to be bounty hunters eager to take me in for a reason I wasn't sure of. I killed them."

"Both of 'em?" Chris inquired, his eyebrows raised.

"I had no choice. One thing I learned from the Gypsies was to defend myself. I guess I didn't do so good last night on Boot Hill, but I'm still alive. With those two bounty hunters, the sheriff of Larengo called it self-defense. I think now maybe those men wanted to collect the money Dugger offered. Anyway, I went by the name of Cal Turner in every town. In the tribe I was called Calarasi Turnovo. Kolarosa named me."

"You are one bag full of surprises, Abel," Denise said, chuckling.

"What are the names of the men in town you mentioned?" Abel asked her father.

"When they talked among theirselves, the dude was called Brad Vishu, the handsome one with the bushy hair an' the mean eyes was called Killer Mason, an' the third man was called Scabby Thorn. They all brought their horses in for new shoes at the same time. I obliged 'em, but I figured they wanted to cover their tracks for some reason, and that the old shoes on their horses would be too easy to trace."

"What did you do with the old shoes?" Abel asked.

"I kept 'em just in case my hunch was right."

"Did you find any telltale marks on the shoes?"

"I reckon there was some marks, but they was marks resultin' from wear an' tear," Chris said.

"Marks that could be identified?" Abel inquired.

"Any marks can be identified, son. One shoe had a calk missin' at the toe. It could have been kicked off travelin' on rocky ground, hilly ground. Another shoe had two nails missin' an' the holes was filled with hard-tamped brown clay."

"Did you say brown clay?" Abel asked.

"Yeah, almost black. There ain't none of that around here."

"I traveled a lot with the Gypsies, sir—"

"Get off your high horse, Abel, if you are Abel, an' quit callin' me *sir*. Call me Chris like everybody else."

"What I want to say, Chris, is that the dark brown clay is peculiar. The only place I saw that was on this trail that leads across the Mexican border. I think most owlhooters on the run travel that way."

"You mean to tell me them fellers is crooks?" Chris asked.

"I didn't say they were crooks, Chris. Other men use that trail. I've never seen the men you speak of—not that I know of," Abel said.

"They been stickin' close to the gospel in town here. I ain't never heard nobody fault them. They've got

Dugger worried, though. He's havin' 'em watched by his special Committee for Community Tranquility."

"That's a jawbreaker," Abel said. "Who is on this tranquility committee, Chris? It sounds like a group of vigilantes to me."

"I reckon you could call it that. It keeps things tranquil for Max Dugger an' the town lets it ride. You could call Silverado a docile town, cowed by lethal authority."

"Don't you mean legal authority?" Abel corrected him.

"I mean what I said, lethal authority. You're a big man, Abel Fargo. I never figured on Joshua havin' sons your size. I wouldn't pick you for a Fargo lest I was told like now."

"That's fine," Abel said.

"I wouldn't take you for a Fargo myself," Denise said.

"Believe me, I am a Fargo, Chris. My mind's unblocked enough so I can tell you things that only a Fargo would know. I remember my father with his dark beard and his deep voice. And his hellfire preaching. Some people didn't like my father, and some did. But he stuck to his guns."

"Guns without bullets," Chris snorted. "I ain't no heathen, but sometimes your pa laid it on too thick for me. It sure surprised me when he fought Dugger's men off when they tried to dispossess him from the Circle-F."

"I was too young then to understand what it was all about. One thing I remember is that none of the townfolk came to help him."

"Dugger had legal papers he was tryin' to serve," Chris said.

"Are you sure they were legal? Even if they were, the honest people in the town owed my father something."

"Son, they figured they didn't owe him their lives."

"You're excusing yourself, Pa," Denise charged.

Chris turned his eyes away. "A man has to look after his own, Denny. The committee threatened to kill the kin of any man who interfered with them. I didn't want you girls hurt. I figured that Joshua would live by his preachin', turn the other cheek, an' fight the thing out in court. Instead, the fire put an end to the whole business."

"Not the final end, Chris," Abel said grimly. "I aim to write the final amen myself."

"Pa," Denise said gravely, "the fact that you didn't help the Fargos in their need has been on your conscience long enough. Here's a chance to make some amends by helping Abel some more."

"I reckon you're right, Denny. What can I do?"

"Abel has to stay here until his strength comes back. In the meantime learn what you can about the three strangers in town. Get their confidence. Then arrange for them to meet with Abel at the old, abandoned mill."

Abel added a note of caution. "Don't let on to anybody, not even your ma, my real name. Until this thing is settled, I'm Cal Turner. Understand?"

CHAPTER FIVE

Several days had passed. Three men hunkered down on rickety benches around the flat grinding stone of the abandoned gristmill, their faces noncommittal, passed around the fast-emptying bottle of whiskey. There was Scabby Thorn, his hands covered with scales like a speckled trout; Killer Mason, his shock of dark hair curling out from under his flat-crowned hat; and Brad Vishu, a string tie dangling from the collar of his immaculate white shirt. Vishu, with his blond hair slicked across his forehead, might have been taken just for a dandy if it weren't for the aura of mystery that clung to him.

"Are you sure he'll come here to talk, Scabby?" Vishu asked in his soft, slow manner. "This could be a trap for all he knows, an' no gunslinger like you describe him is goin' to walk into a trap with his eyes open."

"Use your brain, Vishu. This ain't no trap. I only seen Cal Turner once down in Larengo. The blacksmith arranged this meetin'. He assured me it would be profitable for us. It won't hurt to hear Turner out. It was hinted he's got a burr in his craw an' money in his jeans. And I ain't give you no wrong picture of him. He's taller than most. Kinda loose-built like a cat. I seen him kill two men who braced him down in Larengo. They was both on their way to hell afore they could get a shot off."

Killer said, "The way I heard it, them hombres was sodbusters who didn't know one end of a Peacemaker from the other. Do you call that a fair showdown?" He glared at Scabby and took his turn on the bottle.

"If them was sodbusters like you say, Killer, then I'm an Apache chief," Scabby said. "Them two rannies started the ruckus, an' they knew what they was doin'. The clothes a man wears don't necessarily make him a sodbuster. Them hombres made a clean draw, but Turner was faster. The sheriff of Larengo, he called it a fair fight. Turner bought drinks for the house. Some said them victims was bounty hunters on orders from Max Dugger, the boss of Silverado. At least that was the rumor."

"Why would Max Dugger want Cal Turner?" Vishu asked.

"He don't. Them hombres made a bad mistake," Scabby said, shrugging.

"If Cal Turner is as fast with a gun like you say he

is, Scabby, mebbe Dugger wants him dead on general principles. Dugger figures he's got the fastest gunslicks under contract an' wants to euchre the competition."

Scabby shook his head. "I ain't never seen Cal Turner in these parts, Brad. If them dead men had some inside know-how about him, they never spoke it out. I figure they was showoffs hopin' the bibby overalls would give them an advantage."

"Were they good enough to be Dugger's men?" Killer asked.

"They wasn't Fester Lomas, from Durango way, an' they wasn't Cy Short. They was pretty good. But Fester Lomas can shoot the eyes out of a hawk at fifty yards with the sun in his face. I ain't never seen Cy Short shoot," Scabby said.

"You probably never will," Killer told him. "If you was loco enough to back him into a showdown, he'd drop you so fast you wouldn't know what hit you."

"You fellers is talkin' through your sombreros," Vishu said. "We ain't got no cause to be worryin' about the speed of random gunslicks. We got our own prowess to be concerned about. So far it's stood us in good stead—we're still alive. We agreed to meet Cal Turner here an' hear what's on his mind. If he's got a stone in his craw, he evidently hopes we'll help him get it out. He's got a grudge against Max Dugger. We ain't got no love for Dugger ourselves." He rubbed his slim gambler's hand across his smooth blond head.

"We can't push Dugger too sudden," Scabby said. "We got to stick with our original plan to build up a rep as innocent citizens eager to help the downtrodden an' the unfortunate an' then make a killin' when everybody is off guard. Dugger owns the bank, remember that."

"Yeah, an' we got money in his bank," Killer reminded them. "I reckon Dugger is suspicious about that money—where we got it an' how. He's a slick operator hisself. He pretends to swallow Vishu's story that the money were left him by an uncle in the Ukraine. He ain't disputin' it until he can prove otherwise. I reckon he's checkin' up on that now, but most people ain't never heard of the Ukraine. He cain't disprove nothin' an' we don't have to prove nothin'."

"Some of that money is honest," Vishu said, "some is questionable, an' the rest can't be traced."

"You're our frontman in town, respected by most people, Vishu," Killer said. "You're sparkin' Dugger's uppity daughter. People cain't figure out if you're a high-rollin' gambler, a righteous Christian, or an honest Ukrainian. Why Dugger lets you get near his daughter I ain't sure. I figure you might learn Dugger's mind through her. On the other hand, she might be connin' *you* for information."

"Don't smirch Irma Dugger," Vishu warned, bristling slightly. "She's an honest female in my book."

"Hey, wait a minute, Vishu, you ain't gettin' serious about the gal, are you?" Killer asked. "I don't know what your book is, but honest females as purty as Irma Dugger is hard to come by. They can talk an honest man out of his virtue an' a fool out of his money."

"Which category are you putting me in, Killer?" Vishu asked.

"Whichever, make your choice. You ain't fool enough to think she's takin' you seriously, an' your honesty is open to argument. Mebbe that makes you a little bit of both, Vishu."

Vishu stood up from the rickety bench, his eyes suddenly cold. "A stupid man's opinions can get him into trouble. Put that in your book along with your other pearls of wisdom," he said softly.

Killer shifted slightly on his bench, but he didn't take his hand off his knee. There was a moment of tension in the air, which was snapped by Scabby Thorn.

"Simmer down, you two," Scabby said, stepping between them. "We ain't here to break up our partnership. I don't fault Vishu for havin' a yen for Irma. Any man would. She's a real purty girl. Mebbe she's followin' her pa's orders to wheedle the truth of our intentions, but that don't alter the facts of life. Our money's in Dugger's bank under Vishu's name. Dugger might urge Irma to marry Vishu so they can get a legal claim on that money. It sounds cheap an' underhanded, but that's the way men like Dugger work. Once married, Brad could be killed an' the money—*our* money—would go to his widow."

"You talk like a man with a paper brain, Scabby," Vishu said. "I'm not marryin' anybody, an' I'm not breakin' up our partnership. Because I'm defendin' Irma doesn't mean I aim to marry her. Besides, you men have my IOU's for your share of the bank account, a guarantee I won't run out with the money. We'll wait here an' hear Cal Turner's story and find out how much money he's got. We might be able to earn an honest dollar before we go for the big strike."

"Vishu is right." Killer Mason nodded. "We'll listen to Turner's proposition before we turn it down. If he's the tiger you say he is, Scabby, we might need him on our side. If he makes us a proper deal, it could be another feather in our cap. From what I gather, most of the people on this range hate Dugger, but they ain't got the guts to blow him an' his gunnies plumb into blazes."

"I reckon that would be an enjoyment we might embrace," Scabby said, "but we might be the lambs who is slaughtered."

"Stop this bickerin'," Vishu said. "We can't make any plans until Cal Turner gets here."

Just then there was a rustling sound outside the opening of the mill—there was no door. A gaunt shadow filled the opening and stooped a little as it entered. The man appeared haggard, his flat-paned features etched with the pallor of someone arising from a sickbed.

He said, in a deep voice, "I'm Cal Turner. Did I hear somebody mention my name?" Bristling with a half-grown beard, the man looked ominous.

The three men stared at the visitor. Scabby Thorn rose slowly from the bench. Killer Mason, his face losing some of its stoicism, dropped the bullet he was fiddling with and didn't bother to pick it up. Brad Vishu kept his long-fingered hands on his knees.

Cal Turner looked at the three surprised men and the shadow of a smile broke the stern lines of his face. He straightened up inside the opening and the peak of his new Stetson brushed the roof boards. The room was hushed for a moment with the impact of his sudden arrival. His blue eyes studied the men before him.

Denise's father, Chris Curtis, had described them well, with a brief history of their backgrounds. Cal had seen their likes before in every town the Gypsies had stopped in. Most of them stopped in towns close to the border and the haven of Mexico just across the line. Chris had told him they were called the devil's disciples.

Killer was the first to find his tongue. "You kinda snuck up on us, Turner. Eavesdroppers seldom hear good about theirselves."

"I didn't hear anything totally bad," Turner said, studying them. "I'm not faulting you for questioning my intentions. If you're honest with me, I'll be honest with you. If you're planning on hanging me up as a trophy, that's another matter. Your pose of damning evil and rewarding virtue isn't about to pull the wool over my eyes. I don't see any halos over your heads. Billy the Kid had quite a reputation for helping the downtrodden even though he killed twenty men."

"Get to the point, Turner," Killer said. "We didn't come here for no sermon about our souls or our intentions. What for did you invite us here?"

"I'm coming to that. Did you hombres ever hear of a family named Fargo?"

"We heard of some Fargos bein' burnt up in a fire," Scabby said. "That happened long ago. We ain't been here long. What about them Fargos?"

"They were my kin, sort of. Let's say Joshua Fargo was a stepuncle of mine. According to what I heard from a drifter in Montana, the Fargos owned the best spread on Apache Creek." The lie came easily to Cal's lips. "He said it was rumored that they were cheated out of their property by a banker who came to town as the heir of the former banker. He foreclosed on all the mortgages that were overdue. The Fargos refused to vacate their property and put up a fight. They were vacated the hard way. By fire. It was rumored they were killed before the fire burned them. I reckon I would have been their only heir if the banker had not finagled them."

"So?" Vishu said, shrugging his well-tailored shoulders.

"So," Cal went on, "I aim to find out the truth here and reclaim the property if it was taken illegally."

"Where do we fit in?" Killer asked flatly.

"That's what this meeting is all about. To find out if you've got the foresight and the guts to take a chance with me," Turner said.

"You ain't even heard our names yet," Killer said. "You don't know nothin' about us. We ain't sure what your real name is. We been traipsin' all through the West from Montana to the Mex border. We know most gunnies, owlhooters, an' bandits. We never heard of a Cal Turner, except for Scabby Thorn, here. He saw you kill two sodbusters down in Larengo. He said you drew so fast he didn't see the action."

"Those men asked for what they got. I don't go around killing people for no reason. Those men were no sodbusters, they were hired guns."

"But you killed 'em dead," Scabby reminded him. "If they was hired guns, they was in the wrong business."

"I killed them in self-defense. The sheriff in the bar attested to that," Turner said.

"An' you bought drinks for the house to celebrate the execution," Scabby said.

"It was no execution, and the drinks weren't a celebration. They were a last toast to the deceased. Let's get back on the track. I know your names from what the blacksmith told me." He pointed to Killer Mason. "You're Killer Mason, the man who fondles a bullet like the one you dropped when I came in. No trouble for me to pick out Brad Vishu with his slick hair and string tie. That leaves only Scabby with his rough hands. Whether those are your right names or not, I don't give a hoot. Names can be changed."

"Like yours? Is Cal Turner your real moniker?" Vishu asked.

Abel Fargo was determined to keep his true identity a secret until the time came to reveal it. For the present he was Cal Turner. He was banking on nobody in Silverado remembering him. The last six years had changed him.

Only Denise and her father knew his true identity and they were sworn to secrecy. He thought of the man who had attacked him in the graveyard. In the dim light that man couldn't possibly have recognized him as Abel Fargo, wanted by Max Dugger. What had become of that man he didn't know, and Denise had been unable to trace him.

"Cal Turner *is* my moniker," Turner said.

"How come you pop up all of a sudden seekin' our help?" Killer Mason asked.

"I'm from up Montana way, sometimes living in Canada. It's just a short amble from Moosehead, Montana, and our cattle sometimes stray across the border. The way the Fargo name came up and their troubles in Silverado with Max Dugger, was because the drifter

I talked to was from Fargo in North Dakota. It turned out that Joshua Fargo, a descendant of the original Fargo after whom the town was named, married Emma Dean and moved to the Southwest to make his fortune.

"Nothing was heard of them for years until the folks in Fargo got word of their death in the burned house. I come from the Dean side of the family. My father's name was Turner." Abel fabricated the story with ease and conviction. It was difficult to think of himself as someone other than Turner. He continued.

"Chris Curtis gave me a good idea of your rep. He said you were men who knew the business of a Peacemaker better than most. He said you had some money, which was supposed to be legal, but he sensed you were eager for more. He told me how you had got the water back for the town of Scotia by eliminating the gang who were bleeding the town white with ransom for every gallon of water they sold them. He told how you had cornered the bank robbers at Thistle and saved most of the town's money. What became of the balance, they never tried to find out. They were happy to get most of it back. Here you've donated to the school board and the church, a thing that's made Max Dugger suspicious, not suspicious enough to charge you with a crime—at least not until he figures out your intentions and whether he can profit from them. Along the way you've got the name of the devil's disciples. How come?"

"I reckon we ain't much for courts an' crooked sheriffs," Scabby said, shrugging his scrawny shoulders. "We've killed men, but they was men who deserved it. We ain't never shot a man in the back, an' we ain't never drawed on a man without a gun. We ain't never put a price on our services, but we accept whatever reward is freely offered."

"Let's get down to brass tacks," Killer suggested. "What do you want with us, an' what can we expect to gain by helpin' you?"

"All right," Cal said seriously, "I aim to get the Circle-F back from Dugger and expose him for a crook and a killer."

"Them charges won't stick in the local courts," Vishu said. "Besides, lawyers an' courts cost money. Lawyers don't study the law to help their clients, but mostly to help theirselves. Once you get tied up in court, they'll bleed you to death. I know. I was tangled up with them once."

"I've got money," Turner announced calmly. "I aim to put some of it in Dugger's bank."

"I reckon he'll enjoy that," Vishu said. "When the bank gets fat enough, he'll rob it himself."

"If he can get away with it," Turner said. "I'll guarantee you an ample wage for your help, with a bonus that might keep you off the owlhoot trail for the rest of your lives."

Scabby let out a low whistle. "You ain't askin' much, just givin' us a chance to get our brains blown out. I ain't never heard of no dead men spendin' bonus money. All the bonus they get is six feet of dirt shoveled in their face."

"That's a bonus every man collects sooner or later," Turner said solemnly. "It's what they do before that final bonus that counts. You hombres are alive because you've got one talent—a fast gun. Right now you're posing as do-gooders, waiting for a chance to make a big killing once everybody is off guard."

"What gives you that idea?" Scabby asked suspiciously.

"I know your kind. Only you're smarter than most. Billy the Kid got a reputation for helping the downtrodden, while he killed twenty men in the process," Cal replied.

"You're repeating yourself," Vishu said. "And we're not Billy the Kid. He killed men fair or foul, front or back, just so they were dead. We resort to killing only when necessary, and when we do, it's face to face."

"There is no such thing as a fair fight, Vishu," Turner said. "The fastest man wins regardless of the purity of his cause. You men have a rep as fast guns. But one day a man will come along who is just a mite faster."

"Turner, you oughta have a soapbox an' the Good Book in your hand," Scabby said. "We all ain't fond of sermons, 'cept mebbe Vishu. He goes to church."

"He don't go for the sermon," Killer cut in. "He goes to spark Irma Dugger, the beautiful princess of Silverado."

"I told you before, leave Irma out of this. I feel cheap usin' her like we are, to get a line on her pa," Vishu objected. "The fact is, I'm not sure she's aware of her father's little tricks."

"Neither is nobody else," Scabby grumbled.

"I know a few things," Turner said. "Chris Curtis and his daughter, Denise, gave me some information on him. They distrust Dugger and deplore the methods he uses to get his way. He doesn't bother the Curtis family because their older daughter is married to Dugger's son, Tony. Tony is cut from the same cloth as his father but without his father's patience and cunning. Tony figures himself something of a gunslick, bullying everyone he can but his wife. Alice twists him around her finger. But that's beside the point. Max Dugger runs this area like an emperor. He demands ten percent of all the increase on each ranch. Tithes, he calls it. He's got a tough crew who go out and bring in the cattle every year.

"He claims the tithes are necessary to cover the cost of policing the range and keeping peace and tranquility. He sells the cattle to the reservations at Xavier and other places, and the army posts along the border, putting the proceeds into what he calls a contingency fund. Nobody knows where that fund is, but it's generally suspected that it's in his own bank account. He's bleeding the ranchers white, but they haven't got the guts to fight back."

Vishu interrupted Cal's recital. "We know all that, Turner. We also heard that he diverted the water that used to run this gristmill that belonged to them Fargos you mentioned. There ain't nothin' we can do about that. We won't be here that long. We aim to make a strike an' scram."

"You men think small and you think stupid. If you stick with me, you'll make more money than you've ever had. I've got money, plenty of it. I own a bunch of stock in the Jackass Mine near Bisbee."

"The Jackass?" Killer asked in a skeptical voice. "How come you was smart enough to grab that stock? Only jackasses would touch it, I've heard."

"It's a long story. The stock was acquired when the

mine showed little chance of paying off," Cal said impatiently.

"If you're rich, why bother with the troubles of Silverado an' the Fargo misfortunes? If you're the fast gun Scabby makes you out, Dugger would hire you at premium pay," Killer said.

"Have you ever heard of vengeance, getting even, paying back the devil his due? I thought I explained. I'm the only living heir of the Fargos. They were robbed and killed by Max Dugger, from all accounts. Crime is a cancer that has to be eradicated before it gobbles up everything in sight. You think you're smart enough to outmaneuver Max Dugger. It might prove to be the other way around. The ranchers are sitting back like scared rabbits while Dugger plucks them clean. Before long Dugger will own the whole valley."

"That ain't no skin off our backs." Scabby shrugged.

"Maybe not, but you could keep your skin and cover it with a golden fleece if you'll back me. You can add to your name as do-gooders if you'll join me. Maybe you'll live up to your reputation before this is over."

"How do you figure to go about all this?" Vishu asked.

Cal turned to Scabby Thorn. "You know the lay of the land here, Scabby. Do you think you could pick me up three or four men who aren't gun-shy and would like to prosper?"

Scabby rubbed his big nose with his clawlike hand. "That won't be no problem this near the border. I cain't guarantee their loyalty past their last paycheck."

"I'll pay them in advance with the promise of a

bonus," Turner assured him. Then he looked at Vishu. "You're sweet on Dugger's daughter, Brad."

"I ain't sweet on nobody, Turner. I've got passable feelings toward her so that I don't want to have her hurt, but I ain't dumb enough to hope my feelings will blossom into affection on her part. What do you expect of me?"

"I'm not out to hassle women or kids, Vishu. I just want you to keep your eyes and ears open, learn what you can about Dugger's intentions and his vulnerable areas. Find out the condition of his bank and what kind of hold he has on the business section of the town. Learn the feelings of the businessmen, the churchgoers, an' all. We want everybody we can get on our side. Your rep as a do-gooder might get them to open up."

"Him sparkin' Dugger's daughter might get everybody to shy away from him," Scabby grunted.

"Maybe not," Vishu said defensively. "The town ain't layin' the faults of her pa on Irma's shoulders."

"What do you expect of me, Turner?" Killer said softly, picking up the bullet he had dropped and fondling it with his lean, supple fingers.

"You'll add some backbone to whatever we undertake. You've got a reputation as a gunswift. You're not averse to using your gun in a showdown, are you?"

"I'm still a-livin', ain't I?" Killer turned to the others. "How about you fellers? It might be we can come out smellin' like a rose."

There was a skeptical agreement on all sides, sealed with handshakes.

"All right, you men know what you have to do. I'll

be gone for some time visiting the ranchers in the valley. We'll meet back here in three days," Turner said, dismissing them.

CHAPTER SIX

Returning to the Curtis homestead on the edge of town, Cal Turner found Denise in the back yard of the house scattering grain for the chickens. She greeted him with a reserved hostility.

"Where did you disappear to, Abel?" she demanded.

Her hostility sparked a sharp retort from Turner. "Just a minute, Denise. I asked you not to think of me as Abel Fargo, not to mention the name even to me until this thing blows over. I'm Turner—Cal Turner. If it got out that I was Abel Fargo, there'd be hell to pay."

"I'm sorry, Ab—Cal," she corrected herself. "I was worried about you. You're not strong yet. If you got into another fight like the one up on Boot Hill, it could be your last. Somebody might recognize you in spite of your red whiskers."

"I appreciate your concern, Denise, but I've got most of my strength back. The beef broth and steaks you and your ma have been feeding me have turned to pure muscle. I'm letting my beard grow until this thing is settled."

"Your knife wounds could break open again," she warned him.

"No chance. I'll see to that. Didn't your pa give you a notion where I might have gone?"

"You've sworn me and pa to secrecy about your business, your name, and your whereabouts. Pa takes his oaths seriously," she told him.

"I can't expect you to side with me and not let you know what I'm doing. I take it you take your oath just as seriously as your pa," Turner said.

"Do you doubt it?"

"Look, Denise, I don't want to quarrel with you, but I have to be careful. As it is, I'm skating on thin ice," he said apologetically. "What does your mother know about me?"

"Very little except that you're a stranger and I took you in. She's a good woman, an honest woman, but I'm not sure about Alice. She might wheedle the truth out of my mother."

"Do you think Alice would expose me if she knew the truth?"

"I don't know, Cal. Max Dugger has accepted her as one of the family and the fact that she's carrying his grandchild has made him especially attentive to her. Tony Dugger is like a buck with tick fever, though. Because of Alice's flirting ways, he loses his temper a lot. Sometimes I think she hates him. I can't understand it."

"You told me she had been more or less engaged to another cowboy who was killed in a shootout in the Palace Bar. You said it was rumored that he was killed on Tony Dugger's orders. That would be a good reason for hating him," Cal said grimly.

"Like most rumors it was never proved. I can't see how marrying him and making them both miserable could be much of a revenge," Denise said. "Let's forget Alice. Have you made any plans for getting even with Dugger?"

"Maybe."

"What do you mean maybe? You've been gone for some time."

Cal was silent for a moment, his strong features solemn in thought. He needed all the allies he could get. Denise had earned his trust and his gratitude for what she had done. But for her he might have died.

"I'll explain it all to you, Denise, because I do trust you and I owe you for what you've done for me," he agreed.

Turner went on to tell her of his plan, the details of which he had not worked out. He told her of the meeting in the abandoned mill.

"I aim to visit the ranchers in the valley who are being robbed by Dugger of cattle he has no right to. His self-imposed tithes have no legal standing. I intend to make a proposition to the ranchers which, with their support, might budge Dugger off his pedestal. Can you think of an excuse to keep me here on your father's Sledgehammer ranch for a while?"

"You can sign on as a cowboy if Pa's willing. We have only two hands, and both of them, Pop Vester and Cap Eby, are getting old and a might creaky. They could use some younger muscle when you get your strength back. Of course, Pa has to approve of the arrangement."

"Of course. I aim to sleep in the bunkhouse. My hours might be a bit irregular."

Before supper, Denise took him out to the kitchen where her mother was finishing up with the cooking. The room was warm and redolent with the smell of roasting meat, boiled potatoes, and steaming coffee.

"Ma, Mr. Turner wants to sign on as a rider while he gets his strength back. Cap and Pop could use some help riding fence and policing the range. Would it be all right with you if Pa gave him a job?"

Letha Curtis, her motherly face flushed from the heat of the stove, put down the apple pie she had just removed from the oven and looked at them. She was still a slender woman with a body kept supple by the activity of ranch life.

"That's up to your father, Denny." There was a note of doubt in her voice.

Aware of the doubt, Denise asked, "What's wrong with hiring another hand, Ma?"

"There's nothing *wrong* with it, but it might cause complications. Your father has certain limitations, Denny."

"I—I don't understand it, Mother. Whatever limitations there are I'm sure Pa can get around them, if you vouch for Mr. Turner. Pa listens to you."

Cal, a little embarrassed by the conversation, said, "If it's a matter of money, Mrs. Curtis, I'm willing to forego any wages. I need the exercise and experience."

"It's not a matter of money," Mrs. Curtis said evenly. "I'm sure you could earn your keep riding range or helping in the blacksmith shop. But any stranger riding into town under foggy circumstances would have to be okayed by Tony Dugger, my son-in-law. Max trusts Tony's judgment. Your father's not in a position to ignore Tony's advice."

Denise snapped, "Are you under Tony's thumb, Ma? It's bad enough Alice has joined them."

"Wait a minute," Cal admonished her. "I didn't come here to cause trouble. I reckon I'm a pilgrim, but I ain't no bounty hunter or troublemaker. I intend to do business with Dugger myself—the kind of business he understands. I'm sure he won't object to my staying here."

"You haven't been around long enough to know the lay of the land, Mr. Turner. Max Dugger has strenuous ways of objecting to what annoys him," Letha Curtis warned him. "He might wonder why you're growing a beard."

"I'm not about to annoy him," Turner lied.

Later, after a supper of steak, potatoes, and garden greens, topped off with generous portions of apple pie and coffee, Turner brought up the possibility of him working on the Sledgehammer. They were sitting in the parlor, Chris enjoying his after-supper pipe. Cal spoke frankly of the conversation he had had with

Denise and her mother earlier, including Letha Curtis's fear of Max Dugger's displeasure.

"You can't fault Dugger entirely, Cal. Every man has shadows in his past that linger to haunt him. I don't know much about Max Dugger's past an' his suspicions of strangers may be founded on cause. If he knowed you was Abel Fargo, he might contrive to make your stay here permanent an' have you planted alongside your folks," Chris warned him.

"Don't ever mention my real name," Cal cautioned him. "If your wife suspected who I was, she'd have a worry on her mind she might share with Alice. I'm not sure whether Alice is mostly Dugger or mostly Curtis."

"Sorry, Turner, I'll be more careful. Dugger an' me is mostly tied together by the baby Alice is carryin' but I don't kowtow to his orders. I don't go out of my way to antagonize him, neither, but if some ranny comes along able to pull Dugger off his high horse, I wouldn't stand in his way."

"I think I can handle Dugger, Chris. My living with Gypsies taught me to read a man's weaknesses and his intentions. Do I get the job?"

"It won't pay much," Chris told him.

"I don't wany any pay. I just want a home base," Turner assured him.

"All right, the bunkhouse is yours. They's a couple of spare bunks down there. Pop Vester an' Cap Eby cook their own chow whenever they feel like eatin'. You'd better take your meals here at the house."

Without saying good night to Denny, who was helping with the dishes in the kitchen, Cal went to take his horse from the corral to the barn and get his gear. To his surprise he found his horse already stabled and fed. His bedroll was gone from his saddle. Curious, he went to the low adobe bunkhouse where a light was burning in the window.

He knocked on the rough plank door and a raucous voice, almost like a raven's croak, told him to come in. He entered the large room and blinked his eyes against the bright light coming from a lantern which hung from the ceiling. The globe of the lantern was meticulously polished and the table, at which the two elderly men sat playing cribbage, was covered by a flowered oilcloth.

"It's about time you got here, young feller," a gravelly voice said. "We put your bedroll on one of the lower bunks."

Turner, his eyes adjusted to the light, paused as he looked at his bunkmates. The one who'd spoken had a grizzled face, sun-baked to a chestnut brown. His ample graying hair was parted on the left and hung down over his right eye. A heavy mustache covered his upper lip and drooped down at the corners. He was shirtless and his exposed red underwear was free of tobacco stains. The other man was clean-shaven with a large nose and deep-set eyes.

"I hope I'm not intruding," Cal said apologetically, "but Chris hired me temporarily—"

"We expected you, young feller," the second man said. "They's plenty of room here. Used to have six to eight hands afore Max wheedled Chris outta the main portion of the ranch."

"What do ya mean wheedled, Cap? That tough gun

crew of Max Dugger's ain't exactly no wet nurses. After the Fargos burned out, five–six years ago, Chris lost interest in the Sledgehammer. Alice marryin' with Tony Dugger sort of put the frostin' on the cake."

"I don't know much about the Fargos or the fire," Cal lied. "I need a place to hunker down for a spell. Denise and her ma put in a good word for me."

"Women is suckers for tall, handsome cowboys. You ain't exactly run-of-the-mill. There ain't much work around here that Pop Vester an' me cain't handle," Cap said with a touch of restraint. "We ain't over the hill yet."

Cal, aware of the older men's feelings, made haste to reassure them. "I won't interfere with your work. I'll find some other way to earn my keep, even if it means working in the blacksmith shop. My name's Cal Turner."

Somewhat reassured, the clean-shaven man said, "I'm Cap Eby an' my pardner is Pop Vester. The only ramrod around here is Chris Curtis hissef—not countin' Denny Curtis. There ain't much a man can do against her stubbornness but give in. She's a mite sorrowful about the Sledgehammer shrinkin' down. I reckon some day, if she has her way, she'll try to build it back up."

"How can she do that?" Cal inquired.

"Don't ask me, I'm just a hired hand. Ask her. It rankles her soul that Alice has went over to the Duggers, especially since the Duggers own the bulk of the old Sledgehammer an' the Fargo Circle-F." Cap sounded rueful.

"More power to Denise," Cal said. "Maybe we can

help her. Thanks for taking care of my horse, men. I reckon I'll hit the hay. I want to get up early and ramble through the valley, sort of get the lay of the land."

"Don't run into no ambush, Turner. Dugger's private sheriff's posse ain't right friendly with strangers," Vester warned him.

Turner slept soundly in the clean, warm bunk. Not a bedbug or cockroach disturbed him. He awoke at first crack of dawn and found Cap and Vester already up with a fire in the small cookstove. Cap was slicing side meat and Pop Vester was whipping up some eggs for an omelet.

"Here I am just crawling out of the blankets and you men are already wide-eyed and bushy-tailed," Turner said, pulling on his Levi's and boots.

"There ain't no sense tradin' the mornin' light for the night dark," Pop Vester said.

"I reckon you're right, Pop," Cal said, proceeding to wash the sleep out of his eyes in the shiny wash basin on the bench near the door.

Without disclosing any of his plans, Cal made small talk while they ate—they'd invited him to share this meal—answering their questions about his past with the white lies that were coming more easily to him. Before he slipped out into the cool dawn to saddle his horse, he cautioned them not to tell Denise where he was going.

"I just want to browse around with no interference," he told them.

Cap cautioned him, "A stranger browsin' around ain't goin' to arouse much confidence. You might be taken for one of Dugger's spies. He uses sneaky ways to get information. Folks might figure you're one of his new recruits, hidin' behind a bristly beard."

"I'll try to correct that idea," Cal promised.

He made up his bunk carefully and stowed his personal things on the shelf behind his bunk in the spic-and-span bunkhouse. He complimented the oldsters on their housekeeping.

"We ain't got no choice, Turner. Denise keeps an eye on the place an' raises hell if we get sloppy," Vester said.

Cal went down to the barn and was dismayed to find Denise there clad in fringed buckskin, stitched boots, and a sombrero. She was saddling his horse. Hers was already saddled. For a moment he was at a loss for words.

"Wha-What's the idea, Denise? Are you aiming to shame me for a lay-a-bed? I had hoped to get away without being seen," he objected.

"When you left last night without even a good night, I figured you were trying to avoid me. I was annoyed by your action and determined to twist your tail. I had a hunch you would ride out alone. The valley's changed since you lived here, Cal."

"But the people are the same," he insisted.

"Not all of them. You're supposed to be a stranger. How do you think they'll accept you without me to introduce you? You go around calling people by their right names and they'll soon be suspicious."

Cal realized she was right, but he didn't want to expose her to any danger he might encounter.

"You could have rousted me out at the bunkhouse," he accused her. "At least I can saddle my own horse."

He finished the job she had started. His pinto was a clean-limbed, deep-chested animal, not showy enough to attract any special attention.

When they were ready to leave, Cal made a comment about Denise's fancy clothes.

"I can't go visiting like a tramp," she said. "I'm Tony Dugger's sister-in-law, you know."

"Do the people resent you for that?" Cal asked as he swung into the saddle.

"I'm not sure. I've given them no cause to suspect me. Where do you want to start, Cal?" she asked him.

On the spur of the moment, Cal was imbued with one desire. That was to see the ranch on which he had been born and raised. He put his desire into words.

"How about starting at the Fargo home ranch? I realize the house is gone, but the windmill, the corrals, and the orchard must still be there," he answered her.

"It's there, all right," she agreed with the shadow of a smile. "Are you sure you remember it?"

"Things are beginning to shape up in my mind, Denise. A look at my old home, even if it is just a burned-out wreck, might clarify things. I recalled the old gristmill my father owned, where I went yesterday to meet the devil's disciples. I heard Max diverted the water that used to run the mill."

"That he did, Cal. He diverted the water onto his north range because he made more money hauling in milled flour and grits on his freight line," she explained.

Cal felt a sense of contentment riding along beside the honest, attractive girl who was caught up in a web which she had had no hand in spinning. She was trying to free herself from a hopeless situation, and he might assist her in accomplishing this. Her sister's being married to a Dugger, and her father's dependence on Dugger's whim, were obstacles of no mean proportions. How he was going to overcome them was still a hazy thought in his mind.

He'd have a clearer view of the possibilities when he met again with the devil's disciples. As they rode along, he became aware of the visible signs of his past; the trails he used to ride as a boy, the fishing holes along Apache Creek. The thought of invading the abandoned home of his childhood depressed him. It would be like waking up from a bad dream that would not go away.

"We're almost there, Cal," Denise said, referring to the Circle-F. "It's changed some since you've been away."

"I know that, Denise. I'm not expecting it to look the same. I reckon even the ashes have blown away," Cal said morosely.

As they neared the land he had loved and grown up in, his pulse quickened and the old surroundings became poignantly clear in his mind. They passed the orchard, which was heavy with apples and pears. Then the site of the burned-out house came into sight, and a shock of disbelief struck him dumb. There was a new ranch house on the site, built of bricks, not adobe, and smooth lumber.

The gabled roof was covered with sawed shingles, not hand-hewn shakes. The veranda extended halfway around the house. A graveled drive, lined with whitewashed stones, led to the entrance. As Denise led the way into the driveway, he got his voice back.

"What in tarnation goes on here, Denise? Why didn't you tell me?"

"I—I wanted you to see for yourself, Cal. Time doesn't stand still. Everything changes—we're changed. I'm a woman and you're a man who is trying to regain his birthright."

"But why did Dugger build right on the foundation of the old house? Does it give him something to crow about?" Cal queried.

"Dugger had little to do with it. Alice is the one who made Tony Dugger build it."

Turner let this sink in. "I don't get it. Sure, Alice and the rest of us had a lot of fun here, but now the fun is nothing but haunting memories. I still don't see why she built here. You Curtises were good neighbors to us Fargos, but you had no cause to be spiteful."

"Wait a doggone minute, Mr. Turner! Maybe it wasn't spite. First look at the practical side of it. The windmill and the well were here. The corrals and barn were still standing."

"I didn't figure the Duggers to be that practical. They don't need a ranch house out here. They're comfortably fixed up in town from what I gather. With a big house on a hill."

"Alice insisted she needed the house to get away from town when Tony went on one of his periodic drunks."

"You mean she lives here?" Cal queried.

"Not now, with the baby so near to term. She stays in the big house on the hill, close to the doctor. Would you like to go in and inspect this place?"

"Isn't it locked?"

"No. There's a caretaker, an oldish man. You might know him."

Cal hedged. "He might recognize me in spite of my beard."

"I doubt it," Denise said. "It might be a good test of your new identity. If he recognizes you, you can swear him to secrecy."

"Is it anybody I used to know?" Cal asked, still wary.

"See for yourself."

They dismounted and climbed the four steps that led to the broad veranda. Stopping at the door with its frosted glass window, Denise pulled the latch string and a bell sounded inside. The door swung open, and Cal caught his breath at the sight of the old man who stood before him. It was all he could to contain himself.

CHAPTER SEVEN

Cal Turner stared at the figure of Herb Condy, fighting to control an impluse to embrace the older man. Herb had been foreman of the Circle-F since before Cal had been born. He had taught him to ride and rope and subsist on hardtack and jerky. Herb was a little older, a little balder, with sadness lurking in his deep-set eyes. Cal's fears that Herb might recognize him were dispelled by the ex-foreman's words.

"Hello, Denny," Herb greeted, planting a kiss on Denise's forehead. "Who have we got here? Another of Dugger's advocates of tranquility? I told Alice not to send them here. I ain't about to disrupt the peace an' quiet of Max's territory."

"Get your hackles down, Herb. This is Cal Turner.

He's looking over the valley with the object of settling down here," Denise told the old man.

Herb gave Turner a hard look and, spitting out a stream of tobacco juice, he said, "I reckon he's a danged fool if he aims to settle here. Have you explained to him about the tithes and the committee, Denny?"

"What's your name, old-timer?" Cal asked, pretending ignorance. "You seem to be making out here."

"I been here most of my life, son. I was ramrod for the Circle-F until Dugger stole the land an' burned the house with the family in it. Alice insisted on me takin' this job lookin' after things here. I ain't nothin' now, not foreman or cowhand. I'm relegated to stable boy an' watch dog. The Circle-F was a proud spread afore Dugger come here with his writs an' mortgages an' six-gun squad. Joshua Fargo was a fair an' respected man, even if he was a mite preachy. He believed in hellfire an' brimstone. Sometimes he carried his personal grudges a mite beyond his expressed tolerance. I cain't blame him for that. He fought for what was his an' his boys'."

"What became of the boys, Herb? Were they burned in the fire?" Cal asked innocently.

"They was two boys. It was surmised the boys burned with Emma an' Joshua, but I ain't sure they found enough remains for four people. I figure one of the boys got away," Herb opined, shaking his head.

"How do you figure he got away, Herb?" Cal asked, submerging his own agitated emotions.

"I ain't sure, but I got a feelin' Abel's alive somewhere, that someday he'll be back to heap restitution on Dugger's head. Dugger exposed his own worry about Abel's escape. He offered a reward for the return of the boy, declaring that he wanted to educate him and treat him like his own son."

"You mean to say the boy was never found?" Cal queried.

"No. The reward still stands. I figure if the boy's alive, he might know something that Dugger don't want made public. Mebbe the boy is smart to stay away. Dugger's got one son, Alice's husband, Tony, who's more ornery an' tough than his pa. Abel would never fit into that Satan's outfit."

"Why did Alice marry Tony?" Cal asked.

"That's a riddle nobody has unraveled, Cal," Denise said.

They cut their visit to the Circle-F short because there was much ground to cover. Good Luck Valley was aptly named by the first settlers. It was watered by the creeks and the Pedro River flowing between the mountains that flanked it. It was a green oasis secluded from the drab desert of mesquite and cactus that surrounded it.

To Cal Turner it was his land, his home, but for the moment he was an outcast from that land. The individual ranch houses were far apart, but the open range was shared by all.

"I love this valley, Denise. I aim to come back here to stay once things get straightened out. Are all the old ranches still here?" Cal asked as they rode along side by side.

"Peter Close is still on the Dipper. Gault is still on the Cowbell. Jesse Malden is still on the Tomahawk.

Morter and Scanlon were swallowed up by Dugger just like he swallowed up the Circle-F," Denise explained.

"One of these days Max Dugger is going to have a bad gut-ache. A man can swallow just so much before he starts puking. I reckon the Dipper is our next stop. I knew Pete. He was a humorous, happy man," Cal said.

"Don't be surprised, Cal, he's changed. Dugger has been forcing the bitters down his throat. I don't know how much more he can take."

When they rode into the Dipper, it looked just as neat and orderly as Cal remembered it. There was, however, a subdued air about the place. Nobody was hurrahing broncs in the corral. The yard was deserted. Cal realized that Pete's boys were grown up and their sisters probably married. They stopped before the vine-covered porch.

"Anybody home?" Denise called out.

She repeated the call before the front door opened and a woman's face appeared in the opening. It was a querulous face, one defensive and at the same time mirroring an aura of fear behind the steel-rimmed glasses. Cal remembered her as a cheerful woman, a purveyer of cookies to the visiting young people. Her dark hair was now streaked with gray.

"Is that you, Denny?" Sarah Close inquired, staring into the bright sunlight.

"It's me, Sarah. We thought we'd stop in and say hello," Denise responded.

"Are you personally escorting Max Dugger's tranquilizers around these days? Ain't it bad enough that Alice is a Dugger now?" Sarah said accusingly.

"You've got it all wrong, Sarah. This is a friend of mine, Cal Turner. He hopes to settle in the valley. I'm acquainting him with the people and the problems," Denise said.

"Come in, come in, Denny, before they see you. No use you getting mixed up in the ruckus. You was always stubborn but fair," Sarah said with lingering suspicion.

They entered the prim parlor with its Navajo rugs, some of which were familiar to Cal. The cheerfulness, however, had gone from the room. No one was pumping music from the oaken organ in the corner, or singing lively songs in the warm kitchen, which could be partly seen through the open door.

"I reckon we came at the wrong time, ma'am," Cal apologized. "I aim to buy me a spread in this beautiful valley. I aim to be friendly."

"That's Max Dugger's song—he aims to be friendly just so we pay our tithes and don't oppose him. Pete's out in the barn with two of Dugger's snoopers. They—they claim Pete's been holding back on his allotment of cattle." Her voice broke and tears glittered in her eyes. "Pete's stubborn, but he ain't no fool. I ain't sure whether he's holdin' out on Dugger or not, but the fact is we don't owe Dugger nothin', not one cow or one cent. He's tryin' to wear us ranchers down an' buy us out for nickels."

"Is that the ruckus you were diverting us from, ma'am? I'll reckon I'll go out and get acquainted with the menfolk. You women can get your gossiping over with while I'm gone," Cal suggested.

Sarah Close gave him a hard look. "You ain't

wearin' no gun, Mr. Turner," she said in a grim voice.

"I'm not buying my way into the valley with a gun, ma'am. I reckon a handshake and a good word should suffice," Cal said, heading out the door before there were more objections.

Cal headed around the house and through the familiar yard toward the big barn. He felt a spurt of excitement and flexed his fingers as he approached the white-washed building. He hoped he would not be called on to match his strength against opposition, but he had to be prepared for it. He had not fully regained his vigor nor his stamina, but there were tricks he had learned from the Gypsies that would compensate for this lack should he be called on to prove himself.

Peter Close, normally a quiet man, would not try to fight two of Dugger's thugs. The fact that Sarah had been distraught to the verge of tears disturbed him. As he neared the barn he heard voices raised in anger and the sounds of a commotion. He quickened his step and slid in through the partly opened door, backing up against the wall as he viewed the dim interior of the barn.

What he saw sent the blood racing through his veins. Two men were beating up Pete! Pete was fighting back against hopeless odds. Catlike Cal slid across the dirt floor.

The two men knocked Pete down, aiming their sharp-toed boots at his ribs. So intent were they on inflicting punishment upon the helpless man, they didn't hear Cal approach. Not until he grabbed one of the men—the bigger one—by his belt, spun him over his leg and into the nearest stall, did they realize they had another contender.

The man fell on his back right under a horse tied in the stall. He let out a prodigious curse that caused his partner to spin around and stare in disbelief at Cal. Taking advantage of the second man's confusion, Cal rammed a fist into his chest. The man gasped as his lungs were deflated. A punch to the jaw sent him sprawling on top of his partner.

The horse began kicking and whinnying. The two men crawled away from the frightened animal. Cal rammed a boot into the first man's head as he attempted to rise. The other man rolled aside and staggered to his feet. Confused by the sudden onslaught, the first man struck out blindly at Cal's weaving shadow.

Cal braced himself as both men squared off to attack him. He was in for a beating, but there was no retreat.

The big, bloody fight continued. But Cal finally stunned the smaller man with hard blows to the arm and the nose. Then he concentrated on the big man's face until the blood spurted. By now the smaller one had recovered a little.

Out of the corner of his eye, Cal got a glimpse of Peter fighting him for possession of the pitchfork. The smaller man wrested the pitchfork from Pete and turned to attack Cal. Cal felt a cold chill go up his spine as he waited for the cruel tines of the fork to cut into him. For just then the big man was holding him. At that moment the drama was punctuated by the roar of a six-gun!

"Let go of him, you scum—and you, drop that pitchfork!"

Cal heard Denise's voice pierce the air. The man had dropped the pitchfork and was trying to staunch the blood flowing from his nose and arm. The bigger man let go of Cal and was cursing in a gibberish of sounds.

"Move off, Tony—hands free!" Denise ordered the big one.

"There's goin' to be hell to pay," Tony said. "Wait until my pa hears about this!"

Cal was still trying to grasp the situation. Denise was placing herself in jeopardy by rescuing him. She had called the big man Tony. He had to be Dugger's son.

Still gasping and swaying from his efforts, Cal said, "Thank heaven you came, Denise. Where did you get the gun?"

"It was laying here in the dirt where it skittered from Tony's holster. I meant to use it, too, if I had to. Now skulk out of here, Tony. Go blab to Max if you want—tell how a girl cowed you with your own gun."

Tony, sleeving the blood off his face, started for the door. "I'll kill you!" he told Cal. "And you ain't heard the last of this, Denise Curtis," he snarled. "Wait until Alice hears of it. You ain't makin' things easy for her."

"She made her bed, let her lie in it. I doubt if you're stupid enough to tell her what happened here. You'd better make yourself out the hero, instead of the rat," Denise cautioned him.

"Come on, Debbs," Tony bid his partner.

"I cain't go no place until my arm is fixed. I'm bleedin' to death, Tony," Debbs whined.

Without a retort, Tony went outside the barn, and the sound of his horse's flying hooves could be heard.

"Come up to the house, Debbs," said Sarah, who stood behind Denise. "You take care of your cowboy friend, Denny."

By the time Debbs's arm was cleansed and bandaged, and Cal's cut and bruised face was tended to, the day was far gone.

Peter Close, none the worse for his struggle over the pitchfork, suggested:

"You might as well spend the night here, Turner. Debbs can ride back to Silverado and make up whatever story suits him."

Cal, not happy with the way the day had turned out, tried to resist the temptation of a hot meal and a soft bed. "I don't want to be a burden, Mrs. Close. My introduction to the valley hasn't been exactly cordial."

"We're staying, Cal," Denise said with finality. "We've got to thrash out this situation. It isn't very rosy for any of us."

Debbs, his bristly face crest-fallen, turned to Sarah. "I wish to thankee, ma'am, fer fixin' me up. You had no call to do that. I deserved what I got. I ain't forgettin' what you done. I got no sympathy for Tony an' my loyalty to Max is measured by my paycheck."

"You can stay and have some supper if you want, Debbs," Sarah offered, not forgetting her western hospitality in spite of the circumstances.

"I cain't do that, ma'am. I reckon the food would stick in my craw. I'll traipse into town afore Tony sends Fester Lomas or Cy Short after me." With that parting apology, Debbs left the house.

After an appetizing supper, spiced with cinnamon and apple pie, they talked over cups of steaming coffee.

"I didn't come here to stir up trouble, Pete," Cal assured them. "It seems like trouble is dogging my footsteps."

"The trouble has been laying there fermenting for

too long, Cal," Denise said. "It's time somebody stirred it up, turned it over, and let the stink out."

"I don't even understand what the persecution out in the barn was all about. I waded in because the odds were unfair," Cal said.

"You could have been tromped on if Denny hadn't picked up Tony's gun and ended the affair," Sarah reminded him.

"Sarah's right, Cal," Denise said. "You still haven't got all your strength back. Tony's a bully. You might have been killed over a few head of cattle. Tony won't take the beating you gave him lying down. He'll get his revenge somewhere in public where his cronies can see you humbled."

"I reckon the future will decide that." Cal shrugged. "What *was* the main cause of the commotion?"

Pete spoke up. "Tony an' Debbs claimed they made a range count of my Dipper brand an' come up with a tally of more cattle than I reported with my tithes. Their count was phony as a wooden dollar. I objected. The range tax, or tithes as they's called, is due next full moon, or fall roundup time. Dugger's collectors, or the Committee for Community Tranquility, are out to humble the ranchers so there won't be no complaints when they steal our cattle. Max aims to freeze us outta the valley by robbin' us little by little. They ain't no virtue in a man hanging onto a no-profit ranch."

"Why don't the ranchers get together and refuse to pay tribute to Dugger?" Cal queried.

"Because it would mean a fight and Dugger has the militia on his payroll," Sarah said.

Cal was tempted to reveal his true identity as Abel

Fargo, but he refrained. Too many people already knew his identity—Denise and Chris Curtis. A secret like that might accidentally leak out. When the time came, he would expose himself, but not before then.

"How does Dugger collect his tithes?" Cal inquired.

"He don't *collect* 'em, we pay 'em," Pete said. "If we renege, *then* he collects them, with an added percentage for his trouble. They was a family by the name of Fargo who lived here. And Fargo refused to pay the tithes. Dugger inherited the bank an' all its obligations an' assets. He had papers to prove that Joshua was delinquent in his mortgage. He tried to dispossess Fargo an' they had a battle at the Circle-F. Joshua stuck to his guns, but then the house burned down with the family in it. That ended that. The ranchers were cowed down by Max Dugger an' his gunnies."

Cal choked up as he listened to the recital. The fury within him was rekindled and he vowed that he would see Dugger humbled, or he would die in the attempt.

"That isn't a pretty story, Pete," Cal said, controlling his voice. "What exactly does Dugger do with the cattle he collects?"

"He holds 'em on his MD ranch, down in the far end near the water, until he gets 'em all together. Then he trails 'em to the reservations, makes a deal with the superintendents, which proves profitable to both sides at the expense of the Indians," Pete explained. "Sells to some army posts, too."

Cal thought for a minute. His plan was sharpening in his mind. "Pete," he said, "don't take any more beatings. Give Dugger's tithe-collectors what they ask. Be prepared to give me a regular bill of sale for the cattle Dugger claims. I'll give you a draft on the bank in Bisbee. Tell Denise or myself just when Dugger will have all the tax cattle accumulated. I haven't got it all worked out yet, but I will have it worked out by that time. I might call on you for help and any men you can trust who aren't scared of a fight. Don't let out what we talked about here tonight, not to a soul. I'll be in touch."

CHAPTER EIGHT

The next morning Cal and Denise were on the trail early. It was a beautiful day and in spite of the lingering sting of the cuts and bruises he had garnered in the fight of the day before, he felt a new exuberance in being alive. He tried to analyze his new feeling of hope and inspiration. The mere fact of being home in Good Luck Valley was enough to raise his spirits, and his returning strength also helped.

Deep down he knew there was something more than the sight of old haunts, his physical well-being, and the eagerness for vengeance that inspired him. That something more was Denise Curtis riding along beside him.

Even with his returning memory, it was difficult to recall their childhood days. But he felt a bit of jealousy that she had preferred Emil to him, a jealousy he immediately suppressed. Whatever feelings were emerging in his mind or his heart could never be realized until the job he had set out to do was accomplished. And there was a good chance that he might fill a grave beside his folks on Boot Hill.

"A penny for your thoughts, Cal," she said.

"I reckon they're not worth a penny, Denise," he said solemnly. "They're just a hodgepodge of trivia."

"Don't you think I should be the judge of that, Cal? You don't impress me as being a man who deals in trivial things. There's something you're holding back from me," she accused.

Her accusation was true, and he made no denial. What he was holding back could not be admitted. Only time and circumstances could prove the worth of his feelings for her.

"Are Asa Gault and his wife, Minnie, still on the Cowbell?" he asked. "I think you said they were."

"If that's what's bothering you, forget it, Cal. The only way the Gaults will leave the Cowbell is in a wooden box," Denise assured him.

"Or in a cloud of smoke," Cal said bitterly, remembering his family's fate.

"Asa is playing Dugger's game, turning over the cattle demanded by Max's tax collectors. The last time I saw Minnie in town, she was bitter. She admitted there was nothing else Asa could do, but she said confidentially that Asa prays every night that some blessed evil, if there can be such a thing, will overtake Dugger and squeeze the last drop of blood from his veins."

"Maybe I'm that blessed evil, Denise," Cal said.

"Evil sometimes destroys itself, Cal," she said flatly.

"But not blessed evil," he said with a smile.

They came within sight of the Cowbell ranch before noon. It was a charming place, with a pond of water fringed with bright green aspens and cottonwoods. Red bluffs rose from the foothills behind the adobe house, a vivid contrast to the white clouds that rode majestically in the azure blue sky.

They rode up the graveled drive that skirted the pond, and they stopped before the house. The place was strangely quiet. Cal noticed the rustle of a lace curtain at the partly opened window, and what looked like the barrel of a shotgun just behind it.

"Asa! Minnie! Is anybody home?" Denise called out in her clear voice.

The front door opened slightly and a shaggy dog emerged, his hackles stiff and his raucous bark echoing from the ledge beyond the pond.

"What's going on here, Asa? Call your dog off!" Denise exclaimed.

The window rose with a complaining sound and a voice came from behind the curtain.

"Who sent you out here, Denise? Your sister, Alice, or Max Dugger hisself?"

"Neither of them, Hank," Denise retorted. "What are you doing in the house? Where's Asa?"

"Who's that stranger with you, Denise? Another of Dugger's persuaders?" the voice behind the curtain inquired.

"This man may be a stranger now, Hank, but he could turn out to be the best friend the valley ever had. Where's Asa?"

"Asa ain't here. Mebbe the stranger can tell us where he is," Hank responded.

"You're talking in riddles, Hank. Can't you shut this dog up? He never barked at me like this before," Denise said firmly.

"This ain't the same dog, Denise—jest looks like Nero. Nero is dead."

The front door opened and Minnie Gault appeared. Her round face, which usually smiled, was drawn in lines of worry. She removed her glasses and wiped her eyes as though to get a better look at Cal Turner. Then she quieted the dog so that her voice could be heard.

"We don't mean to be unfriendly, Denise. Two of Dugger's men were here two days ago. They shot our old dog, Nero, because he attacked them. This dog is one of Nero's pups, grown up."

"They shot your dog?" Denise said in disbelief.

"We're lucky they didn't shoot Asa. They came to remind Asa of the tax he owes and warned him to have it ready—eighty head of cattle. Asa objected to the tax, but he lost the argument. He went out yesterday to tell our range riders, Hardy and Lee, to cut the cattle out. They live in the line shack on the high range near the foot of Miller Peak. He was supposed to come back last night, but he never showed up," Minnie said.

"That often happens on a ranch, Minnie," Denise said, hoping to reassure her. "Do you mind if we come in the house? Cal Turner, here, has something to talk over."

"Forgive me, Denise. I'm so flustered I forgot my manners," Minnie apologized, collaring the dog.

Hank, the hired hand, stood behind her with the shotgun.

The interior of the house was warm and inviting, its adobe walls displaying pictures of Asa and Minnie in their younger days. The flagstone floor was covered by hand-woven rag rugs, and lace curtains hung at the windows. When Cal was seated on the creaky rocker and Denise seated on the faded settle, Cal spoke up.

"I'm right sorry, Mrs. Gault, that we came at such a worrisome time. However, maybe it's good we did come. As far as my association with Max Dugger is concerned, I've already made my intentions very clear to him."

"I'll say you did," Denise agreed. "You not only took the starch out of Tony, you sent him home without his gun."

"You sent him home without his gun, Miss Curtis. If you hadn't come along when you did, things could have ended differently. I was sucking in my last breath, and about to be euchred out of the ruckus."

"Don't *Miss Curtis* me, Mr. Turner. False modesty is a snare and a delusion."

"Whatever that means," Cal said.

"Stop bickering," Minnie admonished them. "Wait until after you're married and can't dodge out."

"You're way ahead of the game, Minnie," Cal corrected her. "According to Denise, she carried a torch for some kid named Emil Fargo."

"The Fargos died several years ago when their house burned to the ground. It's a sad story. Some people still say that one of the twin boys got away, but they don't know which one. I reckon if he did get away, he'd be back by now. I liked them folks, even if Joshua Fargo was a bit unbendin' in his ways. He was a real preacher, you know. The minister we got now serves Max Dugger."

"I've gathered that Max Dugger isn't too popular in the valley. Why don't you folks stand up against him?" Cal asked, feeling her out.

"Because we ain't got no more chance of humblin' him than a snowball in hell. He owns the bank, he owns the law. And there ain't much use in prayin' if it has to through Reverend Meeker. Asa done his share of prayin' an' look what it got him."

"Wait a minute, Minnie, don't give up on Asa. He might show up any minute. We'll keep an eye out for him on our way up the valley," Denise assured her.

Hank, silent until now, spoke up. "I had a notion to go look for Asa myself, but I was feared of leavin' Minnie alone. I didn't like the way them fellers argued the other day. They threatened if Asa didn't pay his tithes an' keep his mouth shut, they'd be back to see that he did. I reckoned they meant to harm Minnie if Asa caused any trouble. I got an idea where Asa might be, but I ain't sure about it."

"Where is that?" Cal asked.

"I reckon he might git Hardy an' Lee to help him round up what stock they could, an' trail it around Miller Peak into them volcanic badlands to the north. They could hide a good-size herd in them ravines an' caves. They's water runnin' and pondin' up in them deep gullies, with grass an' brush for browse to last until after the fall roundup."

"I don't think Asa would go that far without telling me what he planned. You two must be hungry. It's near noontime. Come into the kitchen. We'll have a snack an' we can talk whilst I'm fixin' it," Minnie suggested.

They went into the kitchen and sat at the table covered with flowered oilcloth. While the aroma of frying ham and potatoes mingled with the fragrant smell of steaming coffee, Cal explained his visit.

"I have no love for Max Dugger and his son, Tony," he assured Minnie. "I've heard stories about them. The Fargos were relatives of mine from way up north in Dakota and Montana," he said, and went on with his elaborate lie. He finished with, "I got a notion that if we ranchers stick together, we can topple Dugger off his high horse."

"What do you mean, *we* ranchers? You ain't got no ranch to worry about," Minnie said, her face flushed from the heat of the stove.

Cal casually covered his slip of the tongue. "I aim to have one, Minnie. They say the Fargos were all burned up in the fire. That makes me their sole heir on my mother's side. The Fargos and the Turners got mixed up through marriage, as I said. I aim to learn if Dugger came by the Circle-F legally, and if he had a hand in burning down the house."

"That was long ago. Seems like a hopeless mission to me."

Cal shrugged. "That's beside the point. You say Asa pays his tithes without too much quibbling. That's good. Tell him not to borrow trouble. I've got a plan, Minnie. I'm not sure of all of it yet, but I think it will work. Tell Asa to make out a bill of sale to me for all the cattle he turns over to Dugger. I'll pay for them—cash."

Minnie's face changed to a mask of suspicion. "Where did you get the money, a holdup, or murder!"

Denise admonished her, "Minnie, you have no right to say such things!"

"Simmer down, you two," Cal told them. "She has a right to be suspicious. I'm a stranger to her—I might even be a spy for Dugger, for all she knows."

"Dugger pays out no cash unless he gets double his money back," Denise reminded him.

"Minnie, my money came to me honestly. I had luck in a mine outside of Bisbee. You'll have to take me on faith, for now." He turned to Denise. "I reckon we'd better get going if we want to reach Jesse Malden's Tomahawk ranch before sundown."

"You seem reasonably acquainted with the valley, Mr. Turner," Minnie said inquisitively.

Cal dampened her curiosity. "Denise has been briefing me."

When they were back on the road, Denise said, "What did you mean I had briefed you about the valley? You needed no briefing. If you don't watch what you say, somebody will peg you as Abel or Emil Fargo, whichever is missing."

"When this mess is cleard up, I'll *be Abel* Fargo. Don't ponder on my being *Emil*. It might bring back the heartbreak you must have felt after the fire," Cal warned her."

In his own heart he wondered how it would be if he were Emil. Emil would have resumed the affection he once felt for her. He would have impulsively faced Dugger and Tony, and he might have paid for his rashness with his life. But he would have gone down fighting, without weighing the odds against him. There had to be another way to handle Dugger—a more subtle way that would make Max squirm and suffer before the debt he owed was paid in full.

They saw no sign of Asa along the way. When they came to a wide draw leading up toward the higher mountains, Denise spoke up. "We haven't found any sign of Asa so far, Cal. The line shack where his two riders, Hardy and Lee, hang out is up this draw. We might find Asa there. It's an ample place with water, a barn and corral."

"I've seen it before," Cal reminded her.

"I'm still thinking of you as a stranger, Cal." Denise smiled, leading the way up the rutted, seldom-used road.

The half-familiar road sharpened Cal's returning memory. There were patches of black sage interspersed with bunch grass turning yellow with the approaching autumn. Wild daisies poked their white heads through the grass, and other flowers, too.

"I always loved this place," Denise said softly. "Remember when we used to ride here when E—Emil was alive?"

Cal was slow in responding to her remark. "Yes, it's coming back to me. You and Emil always rode together. I brought up the rear like a tag-along."

"Don't put yourself down, Cal. I think you got more out of the ride than we did. You absorbed the beauty; we just rode through it."

"You two were absorbed in each other," Cal responded.

"Forget about Emil. Emil is dead unless you've been pulling my leg. Emil was lively, he paid attention to me, and it flattered me. What Emil would be like now, I'm not sure. Age brings responsibility and that sobers a man."

They were getting closer to the towering bulk of Miller Peak, and the trees were crowding in about them. As they made a sharp turn in the road, Denise stopped her horse and sniffed the air.

"What's the matter, Denise?" Cal asked.

"Do you smell smoke?"

They had reached a fence built of pine rails. Cal looked through the trees ahead. "I reckon I do. There's smoke up ahead."

"They've probably got the stove fired up. The evenings get chilly up here," Denise said.

"There's too much smoke for that. Come on!" Cal barked, spurring his horse around her.

They rode pell-mell through the brush, taking a shortcut. As they reached the clearing around the large cabin, flames were pouring from the windows and the roof. There was no sign of life around the cabin. Cal rode ahead blindly, a strange sight before his mind and his emotions. He wasn't seeing the line shack, he was seeing the Fargo ranch engulfed in flames—hot, searing flames! His family was in those flames. Strange visions danced before his eyes.

Gunshots punctuated his wracking sobs. He was in the attic again, unable to reach the floor below because of the flames leaping up the stairs. He ran to the window at the end of the gabled roof. He yanked it open. There in the bright light of the flames he saw—he saw—he saw a man running from the house into the trees with a gun in one hand and a kerosene can in the other. A spasm of futility and grief brought tears of frustration to his eyes.

He blinked them away. His vision cleared. The man running from the burning house was none other than Max Dugger!

Cal was about to ride into the flames when a bullet, screaming past his head, shocked him out of the vision. Denise was blocking his way, beating his horse with her quirt to turn him away from the fire.

"Stop, Cal! You're crazy! Get out of range!" she cried.

His horse yielded to the lashing of Denise's quirt. As he turned to round the corner of the building, another shot rangout. He heard a plaintive whimper from Denise. Checking his horse, he put himself between her and the line of fire.

Denise swayed in the saddle, clinging to the horn. Struggling through the haze of his mangled emotions, Cal leaped to the ground and caught her in his arms as she toppled from the saddle. He cursed under his breath as her slim form wilted in his arms. He trembled with fury and remorse. This was a horror he had never dreamed of. It was his fault. He had brought her to this inferno of fire and destruction. He carried her behind the nearby screen of juniper bushes and put her on a soft bed of dried needles.

"Oh, no!" he moaned. "Where are you hit, Denise?"

Her words came, garbled. "In—in my ri—right side."

"The buzzards are going to pay for this! Those hyenas—"

"I—I'll be all right. Whoever shot at us must have recognized us. Watch out for them, E—Emil."

The name slipped out in her pain and bewilderment. Cal ignored it, but it jarred his emotions. It was forgivable in these once-familiar surroundings and with her mind twisted by pain and shock.

He was torn between the need to find their attackers and the need to inspect her wound. Snatching his rifle from the boot on his saddle, he ran to the opposite side of the burning house and stared into the trees from which the shots had come. He could see nothing in the thick growth of chaparral and pinon. He fired off two shots in quick succession, hoping to drive the attacker away.

If he and Denise had been recognized, their future would be in jeopardy. But it was possible they could not be identified because of the billowing smoke. As he was desperately trying to make out the forms of their attackers, Cal heard shots coming from the direction of the hill. Not knowing if the new shots were from friend or foe, he went back to where Denise lay on the bed of soft juniper needles, shielded from the smoke.

CHAPTER NINE

The reality of the situation struck Cal like a stunning blow. Even while the visions, which had haunted him in his first attack on the fire, were still moiling in his distracted mind, his emotions engulfed him with guilt and remorse. He heard Denise's voice. Weak as it was, it penetrated his consciousness and galvanized him into action.

"It hurts, Emil. Don't—don't leave me." There was pleading in her tone.

"Where does it hurt, Denise?" The question was superfluous. He could see the blood on her blouse. It was on her right side, but he couldn't tell the exact location of the bullet.

"My side, my right shoulder," she said in a choking voice.

Cal fought off the realization that she might be dying. He inspected the shoulder. His fingers probed gently for the wound, hoping the bullet would be near the surface. Her low moaning sounds almost unnerved him.

"I've got to sterilize the wound, Denise. I'll get my bottle of whiskey from my saddlebags."

In the smoke-shrouded light, her eyes looked up at him. They seemed clear now but frightened. "Don't—don't leave me, Cal. I'm—I'm frightened," she said brokenly.

"I'll be right back, honey." The endearment slipped out naturally.

As he went to his horse nearby, he heard two more shots, but none came his way. The fire was subsiding in the house, and the afternoon was clearing of smoke. As he reached into his saddlebag, he looked toward the pines up the hill. He saw a movement, but he could recognize no one. He uncorked the bottle of whiskey as he went back to where Denise lay like a wounded doe.

"This is going to burn, Denise. Grit your teeth," he advised her.

He poured whiskey over the wound and, whipping off the bandana around his neck, he wiped the blood away. He poured whiskey over the bandana and repeated the cleansing.

"I'm going to turn you over, Denise, to see if the bullet went all the way through. If it didn't . . ."

She was gasping against the burn of the whiskey. Her eyes were closed.

"Do what you have to do, Cal. Don't blame me if I pass out."

"I'll be gentle, Denise," he promised.

He got the bedroll from his saddle and lay down a blanket on which to roll her.

The blood on her back gave him hope that he wouldn't have to probe for the bullet. He was soon happy to see the bullet had indeed exited through the back. Getting a clean shirt from his saddlebag, he bandaged her as best he could.

But he had to get her someplace where she could be taken care of properly. The hate of the man who had done this to her, welled up like bitter gall in his throat. He straightened up and looked around. The fire had died down considerably, and through a window he could make out the interior of the cabin.

The cast-iron stove was intact but glowing from the heat of the fire. Most of the furnishings were being nibbled to ashes by small flames. He looked at the bunks. The blankets were still smoldering. On one of the bunks there was what appeared to be a man. He clenched his fists. It couldn't be a man. A man would have escaped at the first smell of smoke.

Then, with vivid clarity, the vision he had experienced on his first contact with the fire came back to him. The vision of his folks caught in the blaze of the Circle-F! The vision of Max Dugger fleeing the scene with a gun in one hand and a kerosene can in the other!

He ran toward the charred ruins, looking for an entrance. The puncheon floor was still smoldering. He knew, instinctively, that if it were a man on the bunk he had to be dead. Still, he persisted in trying to reach him. He stepped inside the still smoldering ruins. Without warning one of the remaining rafters crumbled and fell upon him. His last impression was that he must die in the fire like the rest of his family. He let out a hoarse cry and fell unconscious.

The next thing Cal knew, he was being dragged across the ground into the fresh air. Somebody was patting out the flames on his clothing. The arsonists had him now, just where they wanted him. They couldn't let him escape to be a witness to their crime. He coughed the smoke from his lungs and blinked his watering eyes. He heard two voices talking.

"We got here just in time, Hardy. Another minute and he'd have been suffocated. He ain't burned bad, only his clothes. The danged fool ain't got no shirt left, only his underwear."

"Do you reckon he's one of the bushwhackers who started the fire, Lee?" another voice queried.

"I don't know for sure, Hardy. He's a stranger to me. If he was one of Dugger's revenuers, we could recognize him."

Cal squirmed, thankful he wasn't scarred with burns again. He coughed the smoke from his throat and spoke in an urgent tone.

"I'm—I'm all right, fellows. You must be Asa's men, Hardy and Lee," he said.

"That's a fact, mister. Who are you, nosin' around this burnin' shack? Has Dugger got some new men to spy on us?" Hardy said.

Cal didn't answer directly. "There's a man in there

on the bunk. I—wanted to save him," Cal said, sitting up.

"Simmer down, pilgrim, that ain't no man. That's an extra bedroll we keep covered to keep the mice an' dust off."

Cal felt chagrined that his desperate effort had been for nothing. "Hey," he said, diverting the conversation, "where's Asa?"

"He left for the Cowbell this mawnin'," Lee said. "Reckon he should have reached there by noon."

Cal ignored the statement. He didn't take time to explain that he and Denise had left the Cowbell *after* noon. "There's no time to stand here and gab. There's a girl back of those bushes yonder. She was shot by someone hidden in the trees up the hill." Cal rose to his feet, dreading what he might find behind the bushes.

"Good heaven!" Hardy exclaimed. "We wasn't shootin' at nobody in particular. We was aiming to drive the skunks who caused the fire into the open, so we could git a shot at them."

"We've got to take care of the girl at once. I don't know—"

"Who is she? Another stranger?" Hardy asked, interrupting him.

"She's no stranger, she's Denise Curtis," Cal explained, leading the way to where Denise lay.

"You mean Chris Curtis's gal? The buzzards!"

The smoke had cleared away and Cal dropped to his knees beside the prostrate girl.

"I—I'm glad you're back, Cal," she said in a halting voice, but not making the mistake of using his real name. "I thought you might have left me."

"Just lie quiet, honey. I'll never leave you, ever. Hardy and Lee are here with me," he told her.

"You—you mean they shot at us?"

"No, honey. I'll explain later. Right now we've got to get you out of here."

"Put me on your horse, Cal, and keep your arms around me," she pleaded.

"No need for that," Lee said, expelling his quid of tobacco. "We've got a buckboard in the barn we use for haulin' supplies. Me an' Hardy'll hitch up a couple of horses in the corral an' bring the wagon here."

The two men scurried off unmindful of the targets they made for any spying eyes. Cal tried to make Denise more comfortable.

"I'm sorry I got you into this, Denise. I had no idea that things were so desperate in the valley," he said, stroking her dark hair back from her damp forehead.

"Don't blame yourself, Cal," she whispered. "I came of my own accord. Somebody has got to stop Dugger and his tranquility committee."

She lapsed into silence and Cal feared she might have passed out. He tried not to disturb her while in his mind lurid thoughts plagued him. Perhaps this wasn't entirely Dugger's fault. The evil men he had hired to do his bidding might have notions of their own. Behind the protection of Dugger's stringent rules, they might be running an undercover operation. They could be skimming off cattle on the side and selling them to unscrupulous buyers.

The fire in the line shack might have been set to cover up their tracks and point the finger at Dugger. Those were ramifications that had to be investigated.

His mind was still churning when Hardy drove close with the buckboard.

"Lee's staying behind to pick up what's left in the ashes. I'll he'p you with Denny," Hardy explained.

Denise's eyes opened. "You—you ride with me, Cal," she pleaded.

"Of course, honey. Does it hurt bad?"

"I—I don't feel it anymore," she replied.

Cal was disturbed by her answer, but talk would be time-consuming and there was no time to waste. Hardy had made a pallet of horse blankets and sacks on the floor of the buckboard.

"I'm going to lift you, Denise," Cal warned her, slipping his arms under her. "Put my blankets on the wagon and keep one to put over her," he told Hardy.

Tying their saddle horses on the back of the wagon, Cal got on the buckboard beside Denise while Hardy did the driving.

"Where's the closest place to take her, Hardy?" Cal asked.

"I reckon it's the Tomahawk. Ollie Malden can help her. She's the best next thing to Doc Haige—specially if the doc's been hittin' the bottle."

They headed down the rutted road, Cal supporting Denise against the shocks as best he could. They reached the main road and headed north toward the Tomahawk ranch. He recalled familiar landmarks as the buckboard swayed and rattled. He wondered if Asa had made it home or if he had fallen prey to the ambushers.

The sun was low in the west when they reached the Tomahawk. The sight of the arched entrance Jesse

Malden had built, with a tomahawk nailed to the arch, brought back memories of Jesse and his wife, Ollie. He recalled Ollie as a big, raw-boned woman with a healthy, twangy voice which she blamed on her Kansas upbringing.

Jesse he remembered as being on the bulgy side with a round, smooth face radiating good humor.

Denise came to as Hardy stopped the horses and got down to open the gate.

"Where are we?" she asked.

"We're at the Tomahawk, Denise. It was the nearest place to get help. You remember Ollie Malden. She'll take care of you," Cal assured her.

Denise forced a wan smile. "Ollie can cure anything—a chicken, a cow, or a person."

Her effort at humor buoyed Cal's feelings, and Ollie's hearty welcome brought back memories of how he had stopped there when riding the range as a youth. There was no limit to her hospitality. Ollie carried Denise into the house with her strong arms while she rattled off questions about their deplorable situation.

Cal and Hardy supplied the answers to her questions. She accepted Cal as a stranger with his bristly beard and added size and maturity.

Hardy excused himself to drive back to the burned line shack and help Lee make a place in the toolshed where they could sleep and live until Asa made up his mind about rebuilding the main cabin.

Cal helped Ollie clean and cauterize Denise's wounds. Denise withstood the operation with stocal courage.

"Do you think I'd better hightail it to town and get Doc Haige?" Cal asked.

Before Ollie could reply, the door opened and Jesse Malden came from the corrals. Scotty Malden, their grown son, came in with him. Cal remembered Scotty as being about his own age when they were boys. He remembered another son, Paul, older than Scotty. Jesse heard Cal's suggestion about Doc Haige and it was he who answered it.

"By the time you got to town, stranger, Doc Haige would be half through his evening bottle. What brings you here, an' what happened to Denny?" Jesse inquired, his fleshy face concerned.

Cal explained his mission in the valley, leaving his relationship with the Fargos out of it for the present.

"If you came to Good Luck Valley to settle down, your education has been sorely neglected. How come Denise is wounded, an' your face is scratched an' bruised? You musta got your first lesson along the way," Scotty opined. "That's a sample of the good luck you'll get here in Dugger's domain. Ain't Denise told you how things is here?"

Denise had recovered enough to speak up. "This is Cal Turner. He's a distant relative of the Fargos, according to him. He came here hoping to claim the Circle-F ranch as the Fargos' next of kin. He knows how things are, but he's not running away. We had a run-in with Dugger men at the Dipper yesterday. One of the men was Tony Dugger. He and his partner got the worst of the argument and Tony ran off leaving his hat and gun behind him."

"Thanks to you, Denise," Cal said.

They told about the fight in detail and about the fire at the line shack, while Ollie prepared supper.

When they had finished eating, it was getting late. Paul, the older Malden son, came through the door as Ollie was clearing the table. He was a husky young man, over six feet tall, with sandy hair and light blue eyes.

"What's goin' on here? How come Denise is lyin' on the couch in the parlor?" Paul asked, tossing his tall hat at a nail on the far wall.

Cal gave him a sketchy story of what had happened up to now.

Paul pounded his big fist into his open palm.

"Somethin's gotta break around here damned soon, even if it means open warfare!" he exploded.

"Let's hope it won't come to that," Cal said. "I've got a plan to step on Dugger's toes so hard he won't be able to wear his boots." He went on to ask them, as he had asked Peter Close, to give him a bill of sale for all the cattle Dugger's tax collectors demanded. He explained his financial position and assured them of payment for the cattle. Then he discussed his plan a little.

"How you gonna pull that off?" Jesse asked querulously.

"I ain't quite sure yet, but I've got angles. What I want is your promise to cooperate with me in the showdown. I ain't askin' you to die, just to stand united behind me."

"With Dugger's gunnies standin' in front of us, is that it?" Paul asked.

"There ain't going to be any tranquility in this valley, with or without the committee, if we don't show some resistance," Cal warned them.

"How come you're so eager to fight Dugger? You ain't even got no land or cattle to protect," Scotty said. "Just that claim from distant relatives."

"I aim to have my own land and cattle, a wife and kids and a home here. I'm riding toward town tonight. I've got to see Max Dugger in the morning."

Cal went into the parlor, followed by the Maldens, and knelt by Denise's side. He aplogized for leaving her stranded. "I've got to see Dugger tomorrow morning, honey. So I have to leave you here."

"I'll be all right, Cal. I'm in good hands here. Take care of yourself," she told him, squeezing his arm with her good hand.

Impulsively, Cal planted a kiss on her warm, receptive lips.

Paul said stiffly, "Ain't you bein' a mite over-friendly, Mr. Turner? We valley folk ain't partic'lar fond of strangers takin' liberties with our women."

"Oh, shut up, Paul!" Denise admonished him. "I've given you no cause to be jealous. Nobody's got a brand on me yet."

Cal felt the warmth of that kiss as he rode toward Silverado in the velvety night. He felt hopeful. Things were shaping up. The Maldens had even lent him a fresh horse to make his ride easier.

CHAPTER TEN

Cal arrived at the Sledgehammer very late. He turned the borrowed horse into the corral, where there was always feed and water, and headed for the bunkhouse. He was too weary and sleepy to rub the horse down.

He found the bunkhouse deserted and wondered where Pop Vester and Cal Eby were. Dropping onto his bunk, Cal went to sleep without taking his boots off.

When he awoke, sun was streaming in the polished window of the bunkhouse. He made no apology to himself for oversleeping. He had earned the rest. He washed his face and examined his bruises. They had faded considerably, for which he was thankful.

Raking a comb through his thick copper hair, Cal

headed for the house. As he neared the open kitchen door, he heard Chris and Letha talking.

"I wouldn't believe it if I hadn't seen it with my own eyes," Letha was saying. "Tony came home the day before yesterday while Alice and me were wondering where he was. His face was cut and his eye swollen. He had no hat and no gun. He swore he was attacked by a mountain lion and dragged by his horse. When Alice doubted him and accused him of being beaten up by a human lion, he blew his top—he struck her."

"In her condition?" Chris exclaimed.

"She promised to kill him for that, so he backed down and fawned on her as he usually does. He's more concerned about his child than he is about her. The strange part is, he was apparently sober. I'd like to congratulate the man who beat him up and sent him home without his hat or his gun."

Cal had heard enough. He walked into the kitchen and confronted Letha. As she stared at him in surprise, he said, "Congratulate me, Letha. But I ain't claiming all the credit. I had some help."

"What do you mean? Where's Denise? She didn't come home last night," Chris said gruffly. "Or the night before."

"Let me explain, Chris," Cal answered him. "Me and that plucky girl of yours went through a corner of hell, and the devil behind it is right here in Silverado." Cal went on to tell of the fight in Peter Close's barn, giving full credit to Denise and Pete for their part in the fight.

"When Denise picked up Tony's gun, Tony hightailed it out the door mouthing curses and a threat to kill me. I reckon he lost his hat in the stall where he fell when I knocked him down. The horse must have trampled it," Cal explained.

"Letha has been staying with Alice a lot when Tony's gone. I told Denise not to follow you, Cal, warnin' her that there might be trouble. She sneaked out, though. Thank heaven she wasn't killed," Chris said, his big hands clenched into fists.

"That's only the beginning of the story," Cal told them. He went on to tell of the fire and her being shot. The news stunned them. "She's all right, though," he hastened to reassure them. "Me and Hardy got her to the Tomahawk in the buckboard, and Ollie Malden took care of her. Denise is conscious and out of danger, but she needs a few days' rest. Paul Malden or Scotty will bring her home."

Chris's face was grim. "Who shot her?" he demanded. "Could it have been Tony Dugger, getting revenge for the beatin' you give him?"

"It couldn't have been Tony," Letha said. "Tony was still at home nursing his cuts and bruises. He's ashamed to show his face in town until the marks have faded."

"Don't worry about my breakfast, Letha. I'll get a bite in town. I've got business to discuss with Max Dugger," Cal explained, going out to the barn.

Cal walked up the familiar street of Silverado past Neola Harper's hat shop, the assay office, and Ed Gaskin's law office. He stopped at Conchita Reva's cafe. People gave him curious glances, but nobody recognized him as Abel Fargo.

Inside the cafe, which was redolent with the smell

of ham, eggs, and tortillas, nothing had changed. The same smells he remembered as a boy. It was late for breakfast, so there were few people in the place. He sat at the counter.

Conchita bustled in from the kitchen, her round face glistening with perspiration. "What for you like to eat? The breakfast? The dinner?"

"It's too early for dinner, senora. I reckon I'll have the breakfast. Make it ham and eggs with fried potatoes and coffee," Cal said.

She had called him a stranger, which was good. He recognized her, having eaten in her place with his mother, father, and brother many times. Conchita didn't serve his food. It was served by a young Mexican girl who looked vaguely familiar. He asked her her name.

"My name is Estrella, but they call me Stella. I am American born," she said proudly. "What is your name, stranger?"

"Cal—Cal Turner," he replied glibly. "I am a stranger here. I don't know anybody."

"You looking for a wife? I'm looking for a husband," she said frankly. "The right kind of man."

"What would be the right kind of man, Stella?" Cal inquired with a twinkle in his blue eyes.

"A man like you, amigo. Are you available?" she teased.

"Why me?"

"Because you're a stranger. You haven't been cowed down by Dugger yet. The men here are afraid of Dugger and his Committee for Community Tranquility. They're a bunch of crooks. They even cheat Dugger, but he don't mind so long as he gets his cut of the spoils. He charges Conchita twenty percent of her profits, leaving her nothing but potato peelings and coffee grounds."

"You mean all the businessmen pay Dugger?"

"They pay or go out of business. Taxes, he calls it. Tony enforces the law," she explained.

"What about the sheriff or the marshal?"

"Pooh! They are puppy dogs."

"I ain't sure I'm the man who can change all that, Stella. I reckon I'll pay a call on Max Dugger," Cal said, managing his food.

"He'll hire you. You're tall, good to look at, and inspire confidence," Stella said.

"You flatter me, Stella. I'm tougher than I look."

"Don't forget about me, senor. I'm looking for a tough man."

"I'll keep you in mind," Cal teased as he finished his coffee and left.

Outside, Cal looked up the sun-baked street. The bank was still there as he remembered it, but it sported a new coat of whitewash. The day was heating up and there were few people in the street.

Cal headed for the bank and entered its iron-clad doors. He blinked his eyes to adjust them to the diminished light of the staid interior. He blinked them again as he spied a girl with unruly red hair at a desk behind the railing near the teller's cage.

Her smooth, slightly tanned skin went well with her violet eyes that viewed him with honest appraisal. Her red lips were parted in a tentative smile. Cal hesitated, remembering the oldster's appraisal of Dugger's daughter as being blonde as butter and just as soft. This girl's hair was too red to be called blonde, so she must be a hired hand.

"Can I do anything for you, sir?" the girl asked, brushing back her hair with a slim white hand. Cal hesitated, wondering what authority this girl had.

"Can I help you, sir?" she persisted.

"I'm sorry, miss," Cal said, removing his hat. "You sort of took me by surprise. I—I didn't expect to find a charming girl ramrodding this place."

"I'm just the segundo, sir. You might say I'm the first line of defense," she told him.

"Do you carry a gun?" Cal joked.

"No, I just have a button under my foot which I press when unsavory characters show up," she said archly.

"Have you stepped on the button?"

"You look innocent enough to me, sir. In fact, you look downright trustworthy. If you'll give me your name and state your business, I'll announce you to Mr. Dugger."

"I figured Dugger would have his daughter here—sort of keep it in the family. I understand his daughter is blonde as butter and just as soft," Cal said.

"I suppose you've heard that she's stuck up and spoiled. Let it go at that. Do you want to see Mr. Dugger, or do you want to travel on?"

"Tell Mr. Dugger that Calarasi Turnovo wants to talk business with him."

"What did you say your name is?" she asked, frowning.

"Calarasi Turnovo—Cal Turner for short," he grinned.

"Quite an impressive name," she said. "I'll announce you as Cal Turner, though. Mr. Dugger doesn't trust foreigners." She rose from behind the desk, looking prim and efficient in her pale green frock that molded her trim figure and set off her red hair. She went through a door, leaving Cal outside.

Cal went to the cage behind which the teller, with gray hair and steel spectacles, was busy sorting money.

"Mr. Dugger picked himself a beautiful secretary," Cal remarked.

"Beauty is only skin deep," the man grumbled. "She can be stubborn where Max is concerned. Quibbles about the way he runs his business."

"Why don't he fire her?" Cal suggested.

"He can't fire her."

"Why not?"

"Because Irma is his daughter," the man said flatly.

"Oh—oh! I heard her called blonde as butter and just soft," Cal said.

"She ain't blonde and she ain't soft," the teller said, adjusting his glasses.

"I reckon not. She hinted that she was called stuck up and spoiled," Cal grinned.

"You'll have to decide that for yourself, mister," the teller said.

Cal went back to the desk when Irma came out of the inner office. "You were pulling my leg," he accused her. "Why didn't you tell me you were Dugger's daughter?" And he thought ruefully how wrong hearsay and people's descriptions of other people often were.

"You didn't ask. You can go in now. My father will see you," Irma told him.

"I met your brother, Tony. You ain't much like him."

"Different mothers. You'd better go in. My father's an impatient man," she warned him.

Cal went into the inner office, hat in hand. The office was typical—rolltop desk, swivel chair, and two Wells Fargo chairs with their open arms ready to trap the unwary. There was other furniture, too, and a stack of ledgers. There was also a Navajo rug in the far end of the room. On top of it was the most magnificent display of Indian pottery Cal had ever seen.

In his travels with the Gypsies, he had run across objects of Indian art but none more magnificent than these.

"What a beautiful display, sir. That is some magnificent Indian craftmanship," Cal said even before he introduced himself.

"I had nothing to do with that. Irma, my daughter, spoils the Indians with the prices she pays for that junk. She insists it takes the sting out of some of the deals we make here."

"I beg to differ with you on the value of the collection, sir. In New York or Boston it would be worth a king's ransom," Cal surmised.

"We ain't in the business of ransoming kings, Mr. Turner. I'm sure you didn't come to admire the display. What's your business?" Dugger demanded.

"Very simple, sir. I'd like to buy an interest in your bank," Cal said calmly.

"You want to do what?" Dugger's eyes widened at the bold announcement.

"Buy an interest in your bank."

"My ears must be failing, Turner. I heard a rumor you were trying to buy a ranch," Dugger said, his poker face regaining control. "Ranches cost money and my bank ain't for sale."

"I've got the money and with me as front man we could take over the entire valley," Cal suggested.

"Hold on a minute, Turner. You walk in here with old Levi's and boots and propose to buy my bank and half the valley to go with it. I'm not sure you know what real money is," Dugger said with mockery in his voice.

"I reckon my offer might sound chancy to a shrewd businessman like you, Mr. Dugger. But I'm also aware that you have a keen eye for business. I've talked to some of the ranchers," Cal said.

"I've got wind of that, too. My daughter-in-law told me that my son, Tony, came home looking like he'd been clawed by some aminal. He said he'd been attacked by a mountain lion, and lost his hat and gun when his horse dragged him away."

"If you're suspecting me of being involved in his condition, you're right," Cal said. "Your son got what he had coming. He and his partner, Debbs, were treating an old man a mite unkindly. He's a bully and a coward."

Dugger became more congenial. "You must be tougher than you look, Mr. Turner. You talk like a tenderfoot. I might warn you not to call Tony a coward and a bully to his face. I'm not defending Tony, I'm warning you. I hire capable men to protect my rights and Tony has to prove that he's as capable as the rest."

"Let the future take care of that," Cal said. "I came

here with a business proposition. How much of an interest will twenty-five thousand dollars buy in your bank?"

Dugger's expression changed slightly. Cal, adept at reading minds through his teaching from the Gypsies, could see the calculations going through Dugger's head. A lot of things could be done with twenty-five thousand dollars. He could make usurious loans with the money. He could even stage a fake bank robbery and claim Cal's money as part of the loot. Cal waited for his cautious answer.

"When I see your money, Mr. Turner, we'll talk business. It takes a lot of brass and guts to run a bank in this frontier country. The ranchers complain about taxes and the interest I charge them on their loans. They don't realize how much it costs to keep the valley harmonious. They pay with cattle for the taxes. It costs money to turn the cattle into money. They pay the interest on their loans with cash. If they lose money one year, they can make it up the next by raising more cattle. If a bank goes broke, it's broke. It can't grow more money."

"Amen," Cal intoned. "I reckon my money will be safe with a shrewd but honest man like you." Actually, he had an urge to slit Dugger's flabby throat.

"You keep talking about money, Mr. Turner. I ain't seen none yet. What's your line? Cattle rustling? Bank robbing? Stage holdups?" Dugger inquired.

"None of the aforementioned, sir. I struck it big in a silver mine outside of Bisbee. I'll get the cash for you. How much of the bank will twenty-five thousand buy?"

Dugger doodled on a paper in front of him. He looked up, his eyes hooded. "Let's say twenty-five percent."

"Sounds fair. Of course, I'll want to look over the books and mortgages and the cash," Cal said with disarming candor.

"Money first," Dugger said. "You'll find everything in order. I'm mayor of the town, you know. I keep the town accounts with the help of my daughter, Irma. She's one of the officers of the bank along with Tony."

Cal forced a smile. "A family bank, eh? I like that, but I'll leave the running of the place up to you. All I'll want is my share of the profits," he said as he rose to leave Dugger's office.

As he went out, he was surprised to see Brad Vishu talking to Irma. Brad cut a figure of gentility in his white shirt and string tie. His brass hair, uncovered as he talked to Irma, was brushed neatly across his head. Cal approached the girl, hoping Vishu would go along with his act.

"I step away for a minute and here you are, Irma, cozying up to a stranger," Cal accused her with a smile. He gave Vishu a warning look.

"What gives you the right to question my friends, Mr. Turner?" she asked archly.

"Call me Cal, Irma. We're going to see a lot of each other."

Irma gave him a questioning look. "You mean to say my father was friendly? He usually suspects strangers."

"He was more than friendly," Cal grinned. "He was downright sociable. We're going to be partners."

"Partners!" Vishu exclaimed. "I reckon your bank is on the skids, Irma. Who is this apparent gentleman that takes over banks so sudden-like?"

"Only a quarter interest," Cal said. "Voting rights."

"Cut the comedy," Irma said sharply. "Brad, this is Cal Turner. You would not believe his real name—Calarasi Turnover!" She mispronounced Turnovo deliberately.

"Just call me Cal Turner. My Gypsy name was decreed by circumstances. Have you got a last name, Brad?"

"I'm Brad Vishu." Brad extended his hand. "My name isn't exactly common, neither."

Cal took Brad's hand. "Glad to know you, Brad. I reckon I can use a few friends around this town. People ain't too sociable—like they were afraid of the plague."

"Maybe we can change your opinion, Cal," Irma said, smiling. She had a disarming smile, and mischief danced in her violet eyes. "Why don't you both come to the house for dinner tonight? I'll send a note to the cook."

Brad and Cal exchanged glances. "I reckon I'd be right proud, speaking for myself," Cal said.

"I'll be there," Brad said. "I wouldn't trust you alone with this pilgrim who buys up banks instead of robbing them."

CHAPTER ELEVEN

Cal was impressed by the Dugger house. It was not pretentiously big but quite attractive. It had a colonial flavor with its four white columns. Cottonwoods shaded it and a cluster of palms stood guard over the green lawn. And a pond of cool water reflected the sky. At the ornate door they were welcomed, not by a servant but by Irma herself.

"Well, I see you're prompt and together. Security in numbers, I suppose. Don't be too awed by appearances. We're common folk here. Come in and get acquainted." She extended a hand to each of them.

Meeting Mrs. Dugger was less pleasant. Irma's mother was aloof and pretentious in appearance. Cal remembered the old man's opinion of her when he spoke to him at the rubbish dump: "Nothing bright about Dugger except his wife with her fancy duds."

Her fancy duds consisted of a long, white dress with no furbelows and a high collar that gave her neck a longish look. Irma introduced them.

"You've met Brad Vishu, Mother, at church. This pilgrim is Cal Turner, a potential partner in our bank."

"I must say, Mr. Turner, you're prepossessing enough to be an asset to the bank. Your beard could stand trimming, but that's a minor matter. You're not a confidence man, are you?" she asked, her tone serious.

He said, "I'm neither robber, murderer, nor confidence man, ma'am. My acquisition of wealth was purely accidental. I inherited it. And I took a liking to this valley, so I hope to put down roots here."

"In the West, sir, roots are usually shallow and temporary. But no matter. Irma's choice of friends has always amused me. At least you're civil and have no barnyard odor."

"Mother, if you hope to match words with Cal, don't. He might expose you," Irma said.

Ignoring the barb, Mabel Dugger said, "The dinner is about to be served. Let's get to the table. Hang your hats on the hall tree."

When they reached the dining room with its candelabra, white linen, and gleaming silver, Cal saw three people already seated at the long table: Max Dugger, Tony, and an alluring young blonde, who was evidently Alice, Tony's wife. When Irma had introduced them, Tony remained seated without extending his hand. A look of pure malevolence glowed in his eyes. Bruises still showed on his face.

"We've met before, the pilgrim an' me. I reckon we'll meet again," Tony said, and his words were more of a threat than a welcome.

"Is this the creature who clawed you, Tony?" Alice asked smugly.

"No one ever clawed me an' lived, and no one ever will," Tony said gruffly.

Mabel, standing at the foot of the table, said, "The dinner table is no place to air differences and extend quarrels. If you people had any manners, you would have remained standing until we were all ready to be seated."

Alice said, "Had I known Irma's guest was to be a tall, handsome stranger, I would have remained in the parlor to greet him. A breath of gentility is welcome in this house after the characters that Max and Tony bring home. Brad Vishu's been tolerated because of his attempts to be civil and because of Irma's interest in him. His intentions are serious enough to lure him into church, which is more than I can say about some people." She looked at Tony.

Max Dugger spoke up, his hooded eyes on Alice. "Talkin' about civility, you might practice it yourself, Alice. Do your back-biting in private."

The meal progressed without further incident, and when it was over, Cal thanked Mabel for the dinner.

"We must accept you, Mr. Turner, if you're to be a partner in the bank. I can't imagine why Max accepted your offer, but Max has reasons of his own, which I neither condemn nor condone," Mabel said.

Brad made his excuses and left with Turner. Irma followed them outside and took Cal aside.

"I want to apologize for my family, Cal. Alice keeps

on needling Tony, but I don't think she means it. I think deep down she must love him. As for my father, nobody knows what goes on in his head. My mother aspires to social graces, with little opportunity to practice them. She can be tough, though."

"Never mind the apologies, Irma. You impress me as honest and forthright, with loyalty to your family, despite their faults. When I become a partner in the bank, we'll have a chance to understand each other better," Cal told her.

"Let's hope the understanding won't lead to more trouble," she said.

As he and Brad mounted and rode down the hill, Cal mulled over Irma's parting statement. Did she really sense trouble? Or was she just trying to sound hard, experienced in the ways of the world?

"Brad," Cal said as they rode across town, "have you spoken to Killer or Scabby Thorn lately?"

"Yeah, I seen Killer. He's loiterin' in town, or he was in town. He made a talk in the schoolhouse on the evils of crime. The kids look up to him. As far as Scabby is concerned, he's in Tombstone recruitin' the men you want to do your dirty work."

"Just a minute, friend. It isn't dirty work I'm aiming to do. I just want to balance the scales of justice," Cal informed him.

"You gave us three days to meet back at the mill. It's three days now and we're still scattered."

"I was a mite impulsive, Brad. Overanxious, maybe. I've got to go to Bisbee, and I'll swing around by Tombstone and talk to Scabby. You an' Killer wait until I return. The Committee for Community Tranquility is out gathering in the tithes, one-tenth of all the cattle. They'll hold them in Dugger's lower pasture until they're ready to drive them to market. We'll start some action then."

"Is it true, Cal, that you aim to buy into Dugger's bank like you said at dinner?"

"I mentioned that when Irma introduced us at the bank. That's why I'm going to Bisbee, to draw out some money," Cal said.

"Ain't that a chancy business, Cal?"

"What do you mean, Brad?"

"I thought you hated Dugger's guts, an' I ain't sure he's not pullin' the wool over your eyes. How much cash do you figure to bring back with you?"

"Twenty-five thousand dollars," Cal said.

"Do you think you'll make it back?" Brad asked. "The Clantons are still operating around Tombstone. They been rustlin' cattle, an' holdin' up stagecoaches. If they got word of your journey, they'd pick up your twenty-five thousand for whiskey money. The Clantons, hidin' behind that crooked sheriff, Behan, are gettin' on Marshal Earp's nerves. He stopped a lynch mob with a shotgun an' made Old Man Clanton furious. He's been robbin' stagecoaches night an' day to keep Wyatt busy. I reckon there's goin' to be a showdown over that way one of these days."

"I'll be careful, Brad. I've been traveling around this neck of the woods for some time. I know trails the Clantons wouldn't bother with," Cal assured him.

"Have you given any thought to the possibility that Max Dugger might send out a couple of trusties to rob you on his behalf?" Vishu asked. "He knows you're goin' after the money."

"Dugger's smarter than that, Brad. He knows if I

bring him twenty-vive thousand he can nudge me for more. Once in his bank, it could disappear and he could claim it was stolen. That way he could evade the law without committing murder. A holdup is always a much more risky business."

Brad shrugged. "It's your show, pardner. Run it your way."

The next morning Cal rode away from the Sledgehammer early. He left a note for Chris, saying he would be gone for a few days. He headed for Tombstone before picking up his money in Bisbee on his way back to Silverado.

It was late afternoon in Tombstone when Cal arrived. As he rode past the Wells Fargo stage office, he saw a crowd milling about near one entrance of the OK Corral. The excitement seemed to spread from there all over town.

Before the Crystal Palace, the fanciest bar in town, Cal spied Scabby Thorn talking to an excited group on the boardwalk. He dismounted and tied his horse to one of the columns in front of the Palace.

"What the devil is all the excitement about, Scabby?" Cal asked.

"What are you doin' here, Turner? You just missed the big bang," Scabby told him.

"What do you mean—big bang? Did somebody blow up the mines?" Cal inquired.

"There was a shootout at the OK Corral. Come inside. I'll buy you a drink an' tell you what I heard from an eye witness," Scabby said, taking his arm and pushing him through the door.

Cal glanced around the ornate room with its arched

mirrors that reflected the crystal-bedecked gaslights. Scabby led the way to a table in the far end of the long room. When they were seated, Cal gave him a searching look.

"What's all the fuss about, Scabby?"

"You may have heard about the feud that's been festerin' between the Clantons an' Wyatt Earp an his brothers. Today it split wide open. The Earps won. Three of the outlaws are dead. The fight lasted no more'n thirty seconds, but I reckon it made a place in history." Then he gave Cal some of the details.

Cal was intrigued by the story. "That must have been a spot of hell," he said more to himself than to Scabby. Now he wouldn't have the marauding Clantons to worry about on his way back to Silverado.

"One thing for sure," Scabby opined, "it defused the tension around here."

Changing the subject, Cal asked, "How have you been making out here, Scabby?"

"I ain't been able to meet your deadline, Turner. Pickin's have been too convenient here with Old Man Clanton takin' liberties with the law. I reckon all that will change now. The fast guns will look for safer pastures. I got some likely prospects lined up."

"I was too hasty when I set that three-day deadline, Scabby. I talked with Brad Vishu and told him to inform Killer to lay low until I give the word. Can I get together with your likely prospects tonight—sorta get acquainted?"

"Where you stayin' tonight?" Scabby asked.

"Where do you recommend?"

"The Silver Nugget Hotel ain't bad. It ain't fancy,

but nobody will give a hoot if we congregate there. The town is restless after what happened. Get a room upstairs in the front where you can watch the street. I'll meet you in the cafe."

Scabby went to round up his prospects and Cal put his horse up in the livery barn. He was lucky to get a room up front in the Silver Nugget. He washed up after beating the dust off his clothes and then raked his copper hair back into some semblance of order.

Then he went down to the cafe and found a table in an out-of-the-way corner. Scabby came in with two alert-looking men who wore no guns. They were poker-faced but had eyes that took in every move about them. Scabby introduced them.

"This here feller is Scarface Smith, an' this other gent is Tom Lender. I told 'em what you wanted 'em for an' they crave confirmation and details."

"Howdy, men. Sit down and I'll explain what I want. I want to rustle cattle," Cal started to explain, but Scarface Smith with a knife scar on his jaw interrupted him.

"We been throwed in jail, nearly lynched, an' got a dose of lead poisonin' for engagin' in such fandangos," Smith said. "If we wanted to rustle cattle, we'd do it on our own."

"Just a minute—let me finish. This wouldn't be rustling, exactly, more like reclaiming them." Cal went on to explain Dugger's illegal system of collecting tithes. "I've seen some of the ranchers in the valley and I hope to see the rest, and I've got them to give me a bill of sale for the number of cattle Dugger's Committee for Community Tranquility, as they call themselves, will skim off their herds. I'm going to pay for them. That technically makes them my cattle. I aim to run them off right under Dugger's nose and lose them in the badlands toward the Mule Mountains."

"That ain't no rosy prospect, Turner. Ain't Dugger likely to have a security guard watchin' out for his interests?" Scarface asked.

"That's why I'm offering double pay, men. With proper caution I think we can ease those cattle out without a fight. If it comes to a fight—well, you ain't exactly strangers to bullets, are you?"

"We ain't strangers to bullets, Turner," Tom Lender said. "We got the scars to prove that. But we ain't invitin' 'em into our parlor, neither."

Cal turned to Scabby. "I thought you said these men were willing to take chances, Scabby. What I propose doesn't require heroes, but it's no chore for yellow-bellies, either."

"Just a minute, Turner," Smith growled, fingering the scar on his jaw. "You are a mite previous with your slander. We ain't backin' off from our word, but we want you to know we ain't no ninnies neither. There's little profit in pullin' the other feller's chestnuts outta the fire. When do we get paid these generous wages?"

"As soon as you show up at an old gristmill near Silverado. Scabby will give you the details on how to get there. I'll meet you there, say—seven days from now. Bring some trail grub along. You might have to wait around there a few days. You'll get your money before you stick your neck out."

"Well, the way I see it," Tom said, "Marshal Earp

is goin' to really bear down on crime in Tombstone with the Clantons off his back. We'll have to find some action away from this vicinity. I'll bring my brother, Lance, along. He can shoot down a nighthawk with his eyes shut."

With his arrangements completed, Cal lost no time in leaving Tombstone in the morning. As he rode out, he saw men digging the graves in which to bury the victims of the shootout the day before.

He headed south toward Bisbee, the road winding through the Mule Mountains, with the boulder-strewn hills and gullies. It was ideal country for an ambush, but until he reached Bisbee he had little to be ambushed for. He reached Bisbee in the early afternoon, stabled his horse, and checked into the Busy Bee Hotel. The lobby was already buzzing with the news of the shoot-out in the OK Corral in Tombstone. He went up to his room, washed the dust off his face and hands, and ran a comb through his hair. Then he had a dinner of steak, eggs, and potatoes, washed down with several cups of coffee, after which he headed for the bank.

The owner of the bank, James Bright, recognized Cal from his previous visit. That was when he took over Kalarosa's account and her mine stock, which the bank still held in a vault. James Bright invited Cal into his private office.

"What's up, Turner? You look like a man with a problem on his mind," Bright said.

"You might call it a problem, a mission, or revenge. Can you spare twenty-five thousand dollars from my account?" Cal asked bluntly.

Bright pursed his lips and let out a slow whistle.

"That's a lot of money on short notice. May I ask why you want it?"

"Mr. Bright, I'm going to level with you, but in strictest confidence. Can I trust you with the facts—personal facts?"

"A bank is like the confessional, son. Nothing said here goes beyond these walls," Bright said solemnly.

"If what I'm about to tell you got out before I'm ready to expose myself, I could be killed—not because I've broken the law, but because it might turn up facts and figures others wouldn't want to have revealed."

Bright frowned and doodled with the pencil on his desk. "You seem tense, son. If you don't trust me, keep your fatal information to yourself."

"It isn't that I don't trust *you,* but secrets shared often get tossed about like dandelion fuzz."

"Is there nobody who knows your secret?" Bright asked, scowling.

"There's two people: Chris Curtis and his daughter, Denise. If anything happens to me, I want them to have my assets. They're working with me," Cal said, looking about as though the walls might have ears.

"What are they working with you on? You talk like a man walking on the edge of a cliff."

"My real name isn't Cal Turner or Calarasi Turnovo. That's the name given to me by the Gypsies. My real name is Abel Fargo."

Bright gave him a sharp look. "You aren't taking me for a fool, are you, son? The Fargos were all burned out years ago."

"Not all of them, sir."

Cal went on to tell how he had escaped and was

picked up by the Gypsies. He explained about his amnesia and his ignorance of his true identity until Kolarosa revealed it to him on her deathbed. He told of his suspicions that Max Dugger had killed the family because his father would not turn over the Circle-F to him peaceably when he tried to evict him with some phony papers.

Bright shook his massive head. "I was suspicious at the time about Dugger's high-handed methods. The former banker, who was supposed to be a relative of Max's, died under suspicious cirmcumstances and Dugger, as his heir took over the bank and started clamping down on the people who owed the bank money. There was a rumor that Dugger had a hand in the death of his cousin, the former banker. The rumor was soon hushed up. Dugger formed a committee to keep peace in the valley and nobody has opposed him."

"I know all that, sir. He bought himself a lawman and he bought himself a preacher," Cal said.

"You haven't told me yet why you want the twenty-five thousand dollars," Bright reminded him.

"I want to buy a partnership in Dugger's bank," Cal said calmly.

"You what?" Bright barked the words. "You've got a cause to hate Dugger's guts. Why in the name of heaven do you want to join up with him?"

"I've my reasons, Mr. Bright. With luck I'll get my money back. If something happens to me, I want to leave a paper here with you. Call it my will if you like. We'll draw it up now with you as executor and you can witness it. What I've got, including the mine stock, goes to Denise Curtis and her father," Cal said.

"If your plans do work out, then what?" Bright asked.

"I'll make different arrangements when the time comes. Just keep what we do here completely confidential. Don't even contact the Curtis family."

CHAPTER TWELVE

The following morning Cal left Bisbee and started through the hills for Silverado with the twenty-five thousand dollars, in large bills, strapped around his waist in a money belt. With the Clantons put out of business in the brutal fight at the OK Corral, other bandits would be cautious for a while.

He had no worries about being held up. The hills on either side of the rough, winding road were almost completely barren, and most of the area's animals were secure in their subterranean burrows.

Brooding over the future and the complicated plans he had embarked upon, Cal was totally unprepared for the bullet that smashed into his horse and dropped him like a puppet with a severed string. The sound of the rifle shot had come from a copse of stunted junipers to his left. As Cal lunged from the saddle to escape injury, he cursed himself for not having taken a pistol with him. He slid his rifle from the boot of his fallen horse and flattened himself against the hot, gravelly earth.

He heard another shot, but this bullet came nowhere near him. He lay still, scanning the hillside for sign of his attacker. Then he saw a man riding boldly toward him, waving his hat. Cal waited for the man to come close enough to give him a sure shot. The man was shouting, his hands above his head. As the man closed in, Cal was startled and perplexed to recognize Brad Vishu riding toward him.

"What the devil are you doing out here, Brad?" Cal demanded, conscious of the fact that the shot that killed his horse had come from the same direction as Brad Vishu.

"You're lucky I did come," Brad retorted. "You can thank Irma for me bein' here."

"What did Irma have to do with it?" Cal inquired.

"She knew, through Max, that you were bringing the money from Bisbee. She told me to keep an eye on her half brother, Tony, and the men he ran with. The roads around here have been plagued with bandits since the Clantons started robbin' the stages."

"The Clantons aren't robbing the stages anymore. Hasn't word reached Silverado about the big shootout in Tombstone at the OK Corral?" Cal asked.

"What shootout?"

Cal explained what had happened in Tombstone. "The Clantons are out of their crooked business. Wyatt

Earp has clamped down on them for good."

"That must have been some fight."

"It lasted only thirty seconds, Brad. You still haven't explained your presence here. Why did you shoot at me? I could be dead right now." In his mind Cal added, And you would have been twenty-five thousand dollars richer. He felt a stab of guilt, suspecting Brad, but he knew little about the devil's disciples. He had only Chris Curtis's voucher for them.

"Just a minute, Turner," Vishu said in a cold voice. "You don't mean you're suspectin' me of tryin' to shoot you?"

"It wouldn't have done anybody any good to kill me," Cal said, ignoring Brad's cold stare. "I'm not carrying any money," he lied. "I've got a bank draft for the money. Nobody can cash it but Max Dugger."

"I reckon you don't trust nobody, Turner," Vishu said. "You made a good impression on Irma. She don't cotton to everything her father does. Tony, she has little use for. I saw Tony connivin' with some of the committee yesterday. This morning one of 'em rode off toward Bisbee. I trailed him. I lost track of him in the chaparral until he got off the shot that killed your horse. I got a shot at him, hit him, too, but he rode off. I came down here to see if you was dead or alive. I think I hit the bushwhacker. I ain't sure."

"Thanks, Brad. I owe you an apology. I'll hide my gear in those bushes yonder. Do you think we can ride double back to town?"

"No offense taken at your remarks, Cal. I never did take you for a fool."

Back in Silverado, Cal went straight to the bank.

Irma gave him a relieved smile. She rose to greet him and held out both her hands. Cal took her small hands in his, and felt a moment of warmth.

"I see you made it, Cal," she said.

"Thanks for sending Vishu out to cover me."

"Vishu? I never sent Vishu out to cover you. I just mentioned to him that I didn't want to see you get hurt, that I liked you," Irma said.

"You trying to make him jealous?" Cal said, grinning.

"He has no cause to be jealous—nobody has, as far as I'm concerned. I'm Max Dugger's daughter. I'm not interested in cowboys, drifters, or disciples," she assured him. "I suppose you want to see my father. It's almost closing time."

Dugger frowned when Cal entered his office. "Well, you finally got here," he grunted.

"I had some business in Tombstone, an' hell broke loose there," Cal said.

"I know." Dugger nodded to the Tombstone newspaper folded on the desk beside him. "There's a detailed account of the fight in the OK Corral. It didn't mention your name, Turner."

"I had no part in it, sir. I went to see a friend in Tombstone. Then I stopped in Bisbee an' picked up the money."

"Wasn't that a chancy thing to do? Didn't nobody bother you on the way down here?" Dugger said.

"I thought nobody knew I was coming with the cash. But somebody must have been tipped off. Someone took a shot at me and killed my horse from under me."

"Did the bushwhacker get away?"

"I'm not sure. Brad Vishu was trailing him and got a shot at him, but he didn't kill him," Cal said, measuring his words.

"How come Vishu was there? Who tipped him off?" Dugger asked.

"He never said," Cal lied.

"Maybe he was the bushwhacker himself. I never did relish those devil's disciples. They're phony, but they ain't broke the law around here. Did you say you've got the cash?"

Cal spread open his denim jacket and displayed his money belt. "It's right here, sir. Before I turn it over and take your receipt, aren't I entitled to inspect your vault and the safety devices to make sure my money is secure? By now the word must have been spread around that I'm investing in your bank. Twenty-five thousand dollars in cash is likely to attract some overambitious gentry. You don't mind, do you, sir?"

Dugger hesitated, then he shrugged. "Stop calling me *sir*, Turner. Call me Max. Come along and satisfy yourself."

The bank was built against a bluff, and at the rear of the office an iron door led into a cave that was hollowed out of the rock. Dugger unlocked the padlock on the door and led the way into the cave. In the dimly lighted cave reposed the big, heavy vault, cemented into the floor. The lock on the vault was opened by turning a dial. When Cal questioned him about it, Dugger explained:

"It's a newfangled combination lock operated by a series of numbers. I'll show you."

"Who knows the numbers?" Cal asked.

"Just me and Irma and the mechanic who set the lock. I'll show you. Stand to one side."

Dugger twisted the dial this way and that, but Cal couldn't see which numbers it stopped on. Soon the door swung open, and Dugger lit a bracket lamp that hung just inside. That lamp illuminated shelves and cubbyholes that held bank notes, gold and silver coins, and various papers.

Cal memorized the interior in one sharp glance. A sly thought entered his mind. Why not strangle Dugger here and lock him in his own vault? Cal curbed his hate for Dugger. Letting him suffocate in his own vault would be revenge, but it wouldn't be restitution. Dugger had to pay, and he had to live to witness the payment.

"You've got an invulnerable depository here, Max," Cal said.

"Count your money, Cal, and leave it here. Nobody can touch it. I'll give you a receipt and sign the partnership papers tomorrow at Ed Gaskin's law office. It's too late to do business today. Gaskin will be gone."

Cal complied with the suggestion without comment. When he left Dugger's office, he found Irma waiting for him. He was impatient to be off, so he was about to give her a perfunctory good night and leave. She intercepted him and offered her hand.

Perplexed, Cal took it and was further puzzled when she left a note tucked in his palm just as Dugger came out of the inner office.

"You ready to go home, Irma? Chuck's outside with the carriage," Max said.

Cal, the note still concealed in his hand, preceded

Dugger and Irma outside where a carriage with two sleek horses waited. Dugger locked the bank door, leaving the old teller inside to tally up the day's transactions. As Cal bid Irma and Max good day, Irma gave him a peculiar look.

"Take care, Cal," she said. "You look tired. What you need is a quiet evening and a good night's sleep."

Cal, still puzzled by her manner, stopped in the recessed doorway of the assay office and unfolded the note she had given him. It read:

> Meet me around nine o'clock in Dagmar Gunther's quarters behind the Palace Bar. There are some things you should know for your own good.

The note was unsigned. Mystified, he crumpled the note and shoved it into his pocket. What could she tell him that he didn't already know? The bank closed early, so he still had time to ride out to the Sledgehammer and report to Chris and Letha Curtis and inquire about Denise.

Hiring a horse at the livery stable, he rode to the ranch to wash up, change to a clean shirt, and join the Curtises for supper. He went directly to the bunkhouse and saw no sign of Vester or Eby. He washed up, changed his shirt, and made his way to the house. He was surprised on tentering the kitchen to find Denise, her shoulder still bandaged, propped in a chair while Letha put food on the table. Chris was visible in the parlor, reading a copy of the *Tombstone Epitaph,* which had come in on the stage.

"Hello, pilgrim," Denise greeted him, her eyes lighting up. "I thought you had deserted me for good."

"For good reason, Denny, but not forever. How are you making out?"

"Oh, I've been taken care of very well. Scotty brought me in. He kidded me along—said he was going to marry me after the roundup," she said.

Cal felt a slight twinge of jealousy, but he stifled it. Emil would have raised a ruckus at her banter. Chris came into the kitchen, the newspaper still in his hands.

"Welcome home, son," Chris said. "I see they had a bit of hell in Tombstone."

"I know," Cal said. "I was there right after the smoke had cleared away."

"I don't know what your plans are, Cal, but I thought I should tell you this," Chris said, changing the subject. "Tony and the committee is still collectin' the tithes, but they're drivin' the cattle to Dugger's north pasture. That's a change in plan."

"How long will they hold them there, Chris?"

"Till they get 'em all 'cumulated. Mebbe a week, mebbe ten days."

"How many will they have?"

"All they can wangle or scare outta the ranchers," Chris said.

"Don't you have anything more to say to *me,* Cal?" Denise asked.

"I got plenty to say to you, Denise, but until I get things settled here, I've got no right to say anything."

"Before this is settled, you might be dead," she said glumly.

"You'll always have Paul to fall back on," he chided her. "Not to mention Scotty."

They finished supper and Cal excused himself without mentioning Irma's note. He rode into town and tied his horse on the rail in front of the ornate Palace. It was nearing dusk and the bracket lamps flanking the door were lit, casting a soft glow upon the white walls and shimmering on the rhinestone sign that hung above the door.

He was unarmed, and he preferred it that way. He wanted no gunplay until the showdown, if the showdown ever came. Entering the heavy door with its frosted glass pane, he slipped in and backed up against the wall. The magohany bar, with its shiny brass footrail, was lined with men. Cal recognized Tony Dugger's tall form, his back toward him.

Tony was flanked by Fester Lomas and Cy Short. All three were armed and had sobering reputations as gunmen. At the end of the bar Cal saw Dagmar Gunther. He faintly remembered her from his boyhood. The years had been kind to her.

She had the same reserved painted face and restless eyes that took in everything about her but revealed nothing. Cal had never been in the Palace as a boy, but he had seen her in the street. Keeping his eyes straight ahead, he walked to the end of the bar and stopped at her elbow.

"Hello, Dagmar," he said boldly.

She fondled the glass she was holding and gave him a quizzical look. "Do I know you?" she asked him.

"I'm Cal Turner. Irma Dugger asked me to meet her in your quarters in the back of the saloon," Cal said evenly.

"So you're Cal Turner. There's been rumors about you spreading in the town."

"Good or bad?"

"Some good, some bad. Scotty Malden was in for a beer after he brought Denise Curtis home. He spoke about you and Denise. Is it true you beat up Tony Dugger and sent him home without his hat or gun?"

"I had a little help from my friends. Tony and Debbs were beating up Pete Close. I didn't like the odds."

"Tony's at the bar with his gunhawks. If you came in here looking for a fight, the odds are against you. If you want to save some blood and skin, you can wait in my quarters until Irma gets here."

"I don't aim to skulk or run, Dagmar, I'm not carrying a gun,"

"I see. If they shoot you, it will be murder, eh?" she suggested. "You'll be dead either way."

"I don't plan to be dead, Dagmar," he assured her.

A ripple of excitement spread across the bar and voices were lowered. Heads were turned in his direction, eyes questioning. Then a man stepped back and raised his voice so all could hear.

"Hey, Tony, is this the one who clawed you an' took your hat an' gun away? Ain't you gonna protect Dagmar?" The man pointed at Cal.

The remark drew a ripple of laughter. Tony's face turned red even under his tan. He moved back from the bar, his shoulders braced and his hand above the butt of his gun.

"What the hell's goin' on here?" he snarled. He faced Cal. "Hey, you at the end of the bar—step away from Dagmar! There ain't no woman here this time to drag your bacon outta the fire!"

Cal stepped away from the bar, his hands raised.

"I'm unarmed, Mr. Dugger," he said in a deceptively soft voice.

"Get a gun or crawl!" Tony barked. "Lomas, give him a gun!"

Things happened so fast, Cal reacted automatically. A gun came flying through the air toward him. As Cal's hand closed around the butt, Tony started his draw. That draw was never completed.

Cal fanned his gun with an invisible motion. Tony's gun was blasted from his hand. Another bullet flicked the hat off his head, and a third knocked the heel off his boot. The room subsided into numbed silence. Tony, driven berserk by the turn of events, lunged at Cal.

Cal was prepared for the attack. With one motion he tossed Lomas's gun to Dagmar and parried Tony's vicious blows. Cal smashed a fist into Tony's square face. blood spurted from Tony's nose, and he backed off for a moment. But only for a moment.

Then Tony started to fight like a madman, determined to destroy this intruder who had made him look like a fool. Cal traded blow for blow with the maniac before him. Both men were taking a heavy beating. Cal had eyes for nothing but his opponent. He didn't see Cy Short push away from the bar, his hand on his gun. But he did hear a gunshot.

Then Dagmar's strident voice cut through Cal's mind. "Pull that gun, Cy, and you're a dead man!" she said.

Cal fought mechanically, gasping for breath, until Tony lay on the floor. He heard the low, excited comments of the voices around him. He fought to stay on his feet and staggered away in a haphazard direction. Then he felt Dagmar's hand on his arm, leading him.

Brad Vishu emerged from the crowd to give Dagmar a hand. They half led, half carried Cal back to her quarters behind the bar. Irma Dugger, who had just arrived to keep her appointment with Cal, helped ease Cal down on Dagmar's sofa as he passed out completely.

"Shall I undress him, Dagmar?" Vishu offered.

"No. Go out front and keep things under control. Irma and I can handle him," Dagmar said.

As Vishu left, Irma inquired, "What happened out there, Dagmar?"

"There's the result of a vicious fight—and he's the winner. They carried Tony off to the doc's office. Let's get Cal's shirt off and wash the blood off his chest. You'll find a man's shirt in my dresser. I always keep extra shirts there, leftovers from my husband, who got lead poisoning," Dagmar said without emotion.

Dagmar got his shirt off with difficulty and Irma brought water from the kitchen.

"I'll let you bathe him, Irma. There's salve and liniment in the kitchen cupboard. You know your way around, honey."

"I'll find it, Dagmar. And thanks. You're the one friend I can count on in this troubled town," Irma said as the older woman left to keep order in the saloon.

CHAPTER THIRTEEN

Cal came to in a room with lace curtains at the window and pictures that stared at him from the wall, shadowed by the subdued light of the crystal shade of the lamp on the table in the center of the floor. He was aware of someone dabbing at his bruised face, which smarted under the burn of liniment and salve. He realized he must be in Dagmar's living quarters, but it wasn't Dagmar's face that looked down on him with concern. It was Irma Dugger's face, at the moment the face of an angel.

"What—where am I?" he mumbled. "How did *you* get here?"

"You got my note. Didn't you read it? You couldn't wait until I got here. You had to get in a fight with

Tony first." She scolded him more out of pity than rebuke.

"Tony got in a fight with *me,*" he replied defensively. "What happened to Tony?"

"They carried him off to Doc's office, unconscious. You were more winded than hurt,"

"I heard a shot. Who fired it?"

"Dagmar did, with Lomas's gun you threw at her. You just made another down payment on your certain demise. Now Tony has to kill you or leave town. It won't be a fair fight next time. It will be a sniper's bullet. I won't be at your funeral."

"I haven't sent out the invitations yet, Irma. You're patching me up. Why?"

"I don't know why. I feel sorry for you, I guess—a lone pilgrim surrounded by enemies. What your object is, is beyond me. Tony has to kill you now, you know," she repeated.

"Your father won't let him kill me. I'm a partner in the bank, you know," Cal reminded her. "I just put twenty-five thousand dollars in his impregnable safe."

Irma hesitated for a moment. "Let's get something straight, Cal. Max Dugger is the only father I've ever known. I was an infant when he married my mother, but he isn't really my father. He treats me like a daughter, and I respect him. But I don't always condone his methods of doing business. It was partly my mother's money that set him up in the banking business. He finagled his way into top saddle. His former wife, Tony's mother, was a dance hall-girl who died under dubious circumstances."

"Why are you telling me all this, Irma, if you're so sure I'm going to die?"

"I don't want you to die, Cal. I like you. Shave off those whiskers and you'd be more than good-looking. Your money in the bank might disappear in ways that could be defended as legal."

"I've considered all that, Irma. And I've never met a girl as outspoken as you, and as attractive." He stared frankly at her smooth face, with a bridge of freckles across her tip-tilted nose and the frame of gleaming red hair enhancing it. "I should be hesitant about trusting your candor, but I feel I *can* trust you. Are you offering me your help, or are you merely warning me?"

"A little bit of both, Cal Turner. Your background's a mystery to me. I can't quite equate you with the name, Calarasi Turnovo. I don't want to see you get hurt. I'll help you if I can, but I still owe my father some loyalty. Just why are you here?"

"I can't tell you that now, but I'll level with you when I can. You can help now by telling me why you gave me that note asking me to meet you here."

"We've practically covered that ground in our conversation. I know Tony. He does most of my father's dirty work."

Her words brought to Cal's mind the vision he had had during the fire at the Dipper line shack, the vision of Max Dugger running from the fire at the Fargo home with a gun in one hand and a kerosene can in the other. Tony might not do all of Max's dirty work. The important crimes Max attended to himself so there would be no witnesses to accuse him.

"Will you take me on faith, Irma?" Cal asked.

"Somehow I do trust you, Cal. You come to Silverado like an avenging angel, but I don't know what you're avenging," she said, dabbing some of the salve off his cut and bruised face.

"To start with, you can help me by giving me the numbers that will open the vault in the bank."

"You mean you want me to help you rob the bank?" she said stiffly.

"No, no, nothing like that. I just want to see some papers that are kept there. I'm only after information," he reassured her.

"First you have to get into the bank. Beesley, the teller, and I have the only keys besides my father. I have my key with me."

"Good," Cal said. "I'm all right now. The beating Tony gave me has worn off. We can go to the bank now. Nobody will suspect us. Tony is laid up and I'm sure Beesley goes to bed early. Max will be home with your mother. How about it?" His words were almost a dare.

"That was a pretty bad beating you took, Cal. Your face is a mess."

"I won't be kissing anybody," Cal said, grinning.

To Cal's astonishment, she bent down and kissed him full on the lips. For a moment he responded, his blood racing. By some strange quirk of his mind, he thought of Denise and wondered if her kiss would be as disturbing.

"There, you've been kissed," Irma said, smiling. "That's one less obstacle to worry about." She gave him the clean shirt. "Here, put this on."

"You shouldn't have done that, Irma," Cal told her. "I can't say I didn't respond to your kiss. I did. But there's no profit in us becoming more than friends."

"Haven't you been kissed before, Cal? By Denise, for instance?"

"Irma, I've accepted you as a true friend. Don't spoil it by petty jealousy. Before I'm through here in Silverado, you might hate me."

"We'll let the future decide that, Cal. If we're going to the bank, we had better leave here by the back door and make our way up the alley."

They reached the bank vault with comparative ease, entering the bank by the rear door. Cal cupped a match in his hand as Irma manipulated the combination lock. Once inside the vault, they closed the heavy door, making sure it was unlocked. Then they lit the bracket lamp. Cal let his eyes roam over the cubbyholes in which piles of papers were stashed.

"What are you looking for, Cal?" Irma inquired, her face looking saintly in the dim light.

"Can you find the papers from the time your father started foreclosing on the ranches around here? I heard they had a fire about that time that burned a family in their beds."

"You mean the Fargos. I was just a kid, but I remember the time. The Fargos had a rather spurious reputation, the way I understood it. Old man Joshua portrayed himself as the self-righteous messenger of God, predicting hell and damnation for all who didn't agree with his ideas. But he himself was some kind of thief. And he wouldn't pay his debts, and when my father foreclosed on the Circle-F, he fought off the men who came to dispossess him, with guns. His wife backed him up in the fight. The squabble ended when the house caught fire during the night and burned the whole family along with it."

"That's not a nice story, Irma. Did the *whole* family burn?" Cal asked, fighting to control his emotions.

"There was nothing but charred flesh and bones left of them. It was rumored one of the boys escaped, but it was never proven. At least if he did escape, he vanished into thin air. We haven't got much time, Cal. Look at the papers you want so we can get out before the night constable comes nosing around."

He sorted out the papers of the six-year-old file and picked out what he wanted.

When Irma expressed an objection to removing the papers, he said:

"As a partner of the bank, Irma, I have the right to examine its records. I'll bring back everything when I've studied them. I can't explain my actions right now, but I'll give you an honest report at the right time."

They locked the vault, and went out the back door. As they were about to emerge from the shadows of the entryway, Irma cowered against him, trembling. He put his arms about her protectively and felt the warmth of her body pressed against him. He stared at the sheds across the alley and through his mind flashed the thought of the man he had fought with in Boot Hill.

If that man was trailing him to prove his true identity and claim Dugger's still valid reward, then he had another problem to contend with. He looked down into Irma's white face that was turned up to him, and he recalled her kiss. His feelings for this daughter of the man he had vowed to destroy were becoming more complicated with every moment.

"There's somebody over there in that shed, Cal," Irma whispered, breaking into his thoughts. "He could have seen us leaving the bank. There's no way we could explain our reason for being here."

"He's probably a range tramp looking for a place to flop," Cal said, trying to soothe her fears. "Nobody would accuse us of robbing the bank. You're the banker's daughter, and I'm his partner."

"Odd things happen in banks, Cal. Sometimes they're robbed from the inside by the people supposed to protect the money," she countered.

Even though he could almost feel her heart beating against him, her words sounded prophetic. Was she warning him against the man who was the only father she had ever known? If so, her warning was superfluous.

Cal counted on Max's making some dishonest move to absorb the twenty-five thousand dollars that he had so innocently deposited for a partnership in the bank. He wasn't actually a depositer, he was part owner of the bank and had to share in its losses as well as its profits.

"Let's get out of here, Irma. If somebody has seen us, they might report it. But they won't stop us."

"You go alone, Cal. I'll walk home from here. It isn't far."

Cal objected, but she silenced his objections. Clutching the sheaf of borrowed papers under his jacket, he reached his horse in front of the Palace and rode out of town unmolested.

When he reached the Curtis ranch house, he was confronted by Denise, who was up and around in spite of her bandaged shoulder.

"What in the world happened to you, Cal? Your face is bruised and greasy with salve!" she exclaimed.

At Denise's loud greeting, Chris and Paul Malden, who'd apparently come to visit, dashed into the parlor. They, too, questioned his appearance. Keeping the sheaf of papers out of sight, Cal explained about the fight with Tony in the Palace Bar.

"I came off with an edge in the fight. I was on my feet—they had to carry Tony out. Dagmar Gunther buttered over my cuts and bruises." He was about to bring Irma into the picture, but he decided to keep his visit to the bank a secret. No use to involve Irma.

"So Tony's laid up," Denise said. "Alice could come to term any day. Ma's up at the house on the hill again. Do you think Tony will live long enough to learn whether it's a boy or a girl?"

"No matter," Chris said. "If it's a gal, Tony will probably drown it."

Cal drew Chris aside and explained, "I can't stay here, Chris. I got things to do and Tony will be gunning for me. He's aiming to kill me one way or another. I'm not even telling you where I'll be, Chris. That way they can't force you to tell where I am. Look up Killer Mason, or Brad Vishu in town. Tell them to get everybody to the old gristmill six days from now."

He brushed aside Denise's objections to his leaving, with a kiss in front of them all. What was meant to be a brotherly kiss turned into a warm, emotional caress that disturbed him.

To gloss over his display of affection, he said to Paul, "Take good care of this girl." To Denise he said, "Don't marry him before I get back."

Cal got his bedroll from the bunkhouse and rode directly to the house Alice had made Tony build for her, on the site of the burned-out Fargo home. It was late when he got there, but persistent knocking got Herb Condy to the door with a shotgun cradled in his arm.

"What do you want this time of night, stranger?"

"I was here a few days ago with Denise Curtis, remember?"

"Did you find that ranch you was damfool enough to hanker after?"

"I reckon I got my mind on one place, Herb. I want to hide out here for a few days. After I stable my horse and rub him down, I'll explain why."

"I ain't got no objections, they's plenty of room. Fact is, I would welcome a little company. I'll keep your secret. Tony would raise the devil if he knowed there was a strange man here. He'd figure you as one of Alice's friends. She flirts to tease him. But it's just teasin'. She's too good for Tony. I don't know why she sticks with him." He sighed.

Cal took care of his horse and brought his bedroll to the house. By the time he got back, Herb had a fresh pot of coffee steaming on the stove. When they were settled down with their coffee, Cal began his story.

"I want your word you'll keep what I'm about to tell you a secret, Herb. My life depends on it. I want you to know how things are in case I don't come back."

"I ain't no blabbermouth, son. But what's all this secrecy business?"

"My name isn't Cal Turner, Herb. I'm Abel Fargo," Cal said bluntly.

Herb's mouth fell open and his eyes bugged out. "You bin eatin' locoweed, son? Abel Fargo died with the rest of his kin."

"Hear me out, Herb. It's a farfetched story I'm about to tell you, but it's true."

Cal went on to tell of his life with the Gypsies, of the fortune Kolarosa had left him. He told of his determination to get the Fargo ranch back and expose Max Dugger as the crook he was.

"Denise Curtis and her father are the only two who know my secret. You might say I'm on the dodge. I've humbled Tony Dugger twice. He's got to kill me or crawl out of town. I don't plan to be killed, Herb. My amnesia is almost gone. A few days here, in the same spot where my folks died, will cure it completely."

"I reckon Denise Curtis will help you, Abel. She's true blue. She still sticks up for your folks," Herb said.

"I know, Herb. I met her in Boot Hill bringing flowers to decorate their graves. She had a love for my twin brother, Emil."

"You lads was dead ringers for each other. How did you prove which one you are, Abel or Emil, whichever you are?"

Cal opened his shirt and exposed the scar left by Emil's wooden arrow when they were kids. "That's my proof, Herb. We were playing cowboys and Indians when we were kids, and Emil shot me with a wooden arrow. I've got to ask you another favor, Herb. Don't call me Abel in front of folks. I'm using the name the Gypsies gave me—Calarasi Turnovo, Cal Turner for short. Will you remember that, Herb?"

"I reckon I can do that, Ab—Cal. I don't know what your game is, but I'll be in your corral all the way."

"It will all be cleared up soon, Herb, if I live. You go to bed now. I've got some papers to look over."

CHAPTER FOURTEEN

Cal was up at dawn the following morning. His sleep had been cut short by his study of the papers he had taken from the bank. The papers puzzled him. Among them he had found a deed to the Circle-F signed by his father in his odd flowery handwriting. He doubted the validity of the signature.

He found an IOU made out in favor of the bank before Dugger had taken over, signed in the same way exactly. Nobody ever signed his name in exactly the same way twice in a row. One of them had to be a tracing, but which one? From the date on the IOU, it appeared the signature on the deed was the tracing. He had to go to the territorial registrar's office in Bisbee to see if the deed had been recorded. He also had to go to the bank and draw out enough money to keep the crew he was hiring loyal to him. To draw money out of Dugger's bank so soon would arouse Dugger's suspicions.

He rode cautiously, keeping off the roads and trails, hoping to spy on Dugger's Committee for Community Tranquility building up the herd in Dugger's north pasture. When Cal reached the vicinity of the north pasture, he dismounted in the thick chaparral and crawled, Indian fashion, to the edge of the bluff overlooking the herd that was fenced in below him.

There was only one rider guarding the herd, Dugger apparently convinced that nobody would question his right to the cattle. Cal estimated the herd to contain five hundred cattle, cattle stolen by Dugger's bold declaration that they represented taxes for the management of the range.

Cal studied the layout of the pasture and surveyed with his eye the land north of the pasture. There was a fence that would have to be cut if he hoped to stampede the herd north. Clutches of chaparral grew on much of the ground, between which the bunch grass had withered in the summer heat. He was not sure how many men he would find at the old gristmill, but even a handful could cut the fence, start fires behind the herd, and drive them to the north into the narrow defile that would spill them out into the volcanic badlands on the other side of the mountains that hemmed in the valley.

He was familiar with the area of hidden chasms, and intertwining gullies and cul-de-sacs from which it would take days to dislodge a herd of scattered half-wild cattle. There were hidden springs in those chasms that watered enough grass to sustain the herd long enough for his purpose. He realized the chances he was taking, but if he succeeded he would make Dugger pay for the evil he had spawned. With that grim thought he rode on toward Bisbee on hidden trails.

In Bisbee Cal searched the records in the registrar's office and found discrepancies even the registrar, who had only been in office two years, could not explain.

"I got no notion of the entries made before I was appointed here by the governor of the territory. Sometimes the offer of money has a way of influencing the integrity of the government appointees here in the West. Some men take these thankless jobs on the reservations or in government posts hoping to steal enough money to make the job worthwhile." He spoke apologetically.

Cal found, for one thing, that the deed he had found in Dugger's bank had never been registered. There had been a mortgage filed against the Circle-F, but the record showed that the mortgage had been paid off. Then the notice of payment had been scratched out.

He next went to the bank and drew out enough money in gold double-eagles to assure the loyalty of his makeshift crew. The next few days he rode around, keeping his eyes open.

Cal returned to the abandoned gristmill on the appointed day, and Brad Vishu, Killer Mason, and Scabby Thorn were awaiting him. Scabby had brought along Scarface Smith, Tom Lender, and Tom's brother, Lance. Cal was surprised to find Asa Gault and Scotty Malden with them.

"How come you're here, Asa?" Cal inquired. "Denise and me didn't see you at the burned-out line shack and you weren't at your place with Minnie when we had a meal there."

"I was ambushed by some snipers on my way home an' had to take a long way around. I'm here because they burned the line shack an' almost kilt Denise. It was all done by Dugger's killers an' I aim to git revenge." Asa said.

"My pa sent me to help out. With Paul spendin' so much time courtin' Denise, I reckon, Pa figured he had to stay with Ma. You've brought a pack of trouble with you, Cal Turner. But you're against Dugger, an' that's a good enough endorsement for me," Scotty explained.

Cal got down to business. He paid the hired guns half their wages in gold with the promise of the balance when the job was done. Then he outlined his plan.

"I checked on the pasture on my way to Bisbee and again on my way back. On my way to Bisbee I saw only one man guarding the cattle, but on my way back I saw him talking to two other men. They were Fester Lomas and Cy Short, Dugger's men. I crawled up as close as I could through the chaparral, but I couldn't hear exactly what they said. It sounded to me like they were going to move the herd."

Vishu cut in. "I heard a rumor in town that Lomas an' Short had a falling out with Dugger. It's possible they were schemin' to steal the cattle theirselves."

"That makes it necessary for us to move tonight. One man will go ahead and cut the wires on the north fence. The rest of us will close in behind the herd. I bought some kerosene before I left Bisbee. We'll start fires in the chaparral, which at this time of year is as dry as tinder. The grass is brown and easily ignited."

"Wait a minute, Turner. It's already gettin' darker than the inside of a boot. My brother an' me, includin' Scarface, ain't familiar with the range here. How we gonna pull off this miracle we're stakin' our lives on?" Tom Lender inquired.

Cal realized the truth of Lender's argument. "Simmer down, Tom," he said. "The pasture is quite a spell of ridin' from here. By the time we get there, the morning light will be filtering over the range. Scabby knows this range. He can go ahead and cut the wire on the fence. The rest of us will spread out behind the herd and stampede them before they start roaming from the bedding grounds. Once they're on the move, we'll flank them and drive them up the narrow wash and over Dead Man's Pass into the volcanic wasteland. Once they scatter into those gullies and ravines, they'll be safe enough for my purpose."

"Jest what is your purpose, Turner?" Scarface asked. "You're a stranger to all and sundry. You've got money which you're spreadin' out like chaff, with little chance of reclaimin' your loss. Only a man with a mind full of hate and a bellyful of sour grapes would stick his neck out so far he couldn't git it back in his collar. We're doin' it for money. You surely ain't doin' it for five hundred head of cattle."

Cal felt all eyes turned on him. He knew that the time for dissembling was past. He was asking these men to risk their lives for a handful of gold. They were entitled to the truth.

"I'll lay it on the line, men," he said seriously. "My name is not Cal Turner. My name is Abel Fargo. I was born and raised on this range."

The men's faces were blank. "So what?" Tom Lender asked.

Killer Mason broke in. "I heard around Silverado that the Fargos were all burnt in a fire."

Cal told them how he had escaped the fire, lost his memory, and was adopted by the Gypsies. He explained how he had gotten his money and why he was determined to destroy Dugger and get back the ranch.

"So you see I've got just cause for what I'm doing. Sure, I could walk up to Dugger and kill him, but that would be too simple," Abel finished.

"You'd have to go through Tony first," Killer warned.

"I've belittled Tony twice, and he's vowed to kill me. That's my affair. As for Max Dugger, I aim to cut him down piece by piece and make him crawl."

"He's got an uppity wife, and a daughter to make a man's guts squirm," Scabby reminded him.

Abel thought of Irma, of her gentle hands salving his face, and of her courage in helping him enter the vault and take out the documents.

"Let's leave the women out of this, Scabby," Abel said firmly.

"I second that motion," Vishu said.

"You oughta know, Brad. You've been sparkin' her," Scabby scoffed.

"Cut it out!" Abel admonished them. "We'd better get going if we're planning to reach the meadow by first light. Have your guns loaded and ready."

Abel led the way through the mesquite and sagebrush. The die had been cast now, and he had involved more than one innocent person in his scheme. If he succeeded, it would be for the benefit of all the valley; if he failed, he would be dead and those left behind would be subject to Dugger's reprisals. He thought of Denise and her folks, who were helping him most. Their only salvation would be the intervention of Alice, whose influence would be augmented by the birth of her child.

They traversed the undulating foothills at the base of Miller Peak, whose nine-thousand-foot elevation blotted out the sky to the west. From there they could look down the valley almost to the Mexican border. As the darkness thinned, they paused in the shelter of a copse of pinon and junipers to rest their horses for the ordeal ahead. There was a water seep there that filled a rock basin with enough water for their horses. The horses nibbled on the grass growing around the seep.

"You ride on ahead, Scabby, and be sure the fence is cut. Once we stampede the herd, we don't want them piling up against the wire," Abel said. "Have you got your fence tools?"

"I always carry them with me. I mebbe could use some help, though."

"You won't need any help, Scabby. Just cut the wire on three–four posts and drag it out of the way."

Scabby took off alone and Abel watched him go, realizing the importance of Scabby's loyalty. The rest of them mounted and followed Abel into the waning night. By the time they reached the gate to the pasture, it was light enough to see the dark outline of the herd huddled together in the far end.

They passed through the gate without incident. There was no sign of the men guarding the cattle. Calling a halt, Abel gave Killer one of the cans of kerosene he had brought from Bisbee. He kept the other can.

"Splash the kerosene on the chaparral and grass along here. I'll go over yonder and do the same. Be ready to light your fire when you see my flare. The wind's puffy, but it's in the right direction."

"I ain't sure this raid is goin' to cook Dugger's goose," Killer complained.

"This raid is only the beginning, Killer. Once we get the herd headed up in the arroyo toward Dead Man's Pass, I aim to go back into town. I've got evidence that will make Dugger squirm. We aren't stealing these cattle. Remember that I've got bills of sale covering most of them."

"Iffen you don't make it back," Lender inquired, "who's gonna pay us off?"

"Contact Denise Curtis. If I die, she gets my money," Abel said curtly.

When the kerosene was spread and ignited, flames leaped up in the chaparral and raced before the wind. Like a huge torch, the breeze lit up the landscape. The herd, sensing the danger, rose into a bawling, churning mass of terror. Abel, with Vishu and Tom Lender rode behind the herd, firing their guns.

On the opposite side Killer, Scarface, and Lender's brother crowded the terrified cattle toward the north. The cattle stampeded into one huge catapult ignoring everything in its path. Abel rode up alongside the herd shouting and firing over their heads. So intent was he at keeping the cattle bunched, he was unaware of shots coming from another direction until a bullet whined past his head.

He ducked instinctively, his eyes searching for the source of this new menace. Had his men turned against him and hoped to kill him and keep the cattle for themselves? Even as he conceived this thought, the flames flared up in the wind and he saw Fester Lomas, Cy Short, and two other men who were strangers to him, trying desperately to stop the stampede. A thought flashed through his mind. The rumor that Lomas and Short meant to keep the cattle for themselves was true!

Abel realized that Lomas and Short had been caught off guard. They were close to the path of the charging cattle. They had to kill him because he had exposed them. He turned his gun on Lomas just as a bullet snatched the hat from his head. His shot smashed Lomas from the saddle.

Short was steadying his gun for another shot. Short's shot missed as Abel's next bullet downed Short's horse. Short dragged his crushed leg from under his fallen mount. Lomas was on his feet, staggering around like a drunken man. The two other men, evidently confused and scared by the fate of Lomas and Short, turned back from the herd and headed toward Silverado.

The terrified herd veered at the sound of the shots and headed toward the west, away from the cut fence. Ignoring Lomas and Short, who were concerned with their own survival, Abel raced ahead shouting for the men on the opposite side to crowd the herd back in line. His shouts were swallowed up by the bawling and pounding feet. He heard more shots behind him as Vishu and Lender were cut off by Lomas and Short, who were fighting for their lives.

The wind changed suddenly, leaping through the grass and chaparral on the opposite side of the herd. Abel, overeager to keep the herd from slowing down, suddenly found the steers converging toward him to escape the new menace of the fire. He was in danger of being overrun and trampled by the sharp hooves of the cattle.

He jerked his horse around and raced with the herd, hoping to keep ahead of them. His horse was weaving and choking in the cloud of dust and smoke that churned about them. By now it was broad daylight, but he could see nothing but the dark cloud and the heaving backs of the cattle who, spurred on by terror, were jostling and careening against his tired horse.

Abel realized that his dream of revenge and restitution could end here under the hooves of a juggernaut of his own design. The herd poured over a shallow cutbank, some of them falling to be trampled by those that followed. His horse stumbled at the edge of the bank and rolled over the edge. Abel held the horse down, cowering behind it with his back against the cutbank. The cattle roared over and around him and then the moment of hell was over.

Choking and bruised, Abel found that he had no bones broken. His horse was able to get up and shake himself vigorously to dispel the dust and muck from his body. Abel mounted and rode after the herd, sparing his horse as much as he could. He was unaware of Lance Lender coming from behind him until he heard his voice, hoarse and strident with frenzy and excitement.

"Vishu's dead, Fargo! Lomas killed him before he died hisself. And I killed Short! The stampede ran over 'em. I managed to ride clear!"

Abel felt the words smash like clubs into his numbed brain. Vishu was dead. He deserved better than that. Abel tried to find consolation in the fact that the dead were men who had lived by the gun, and had died by the gun. It was foreordained, but he felt no triumph in the fact that he had been the instigator of their demise.

He rode on blindly having no words to condone or accuse Lance Lender for what was done. He followed the trail of dust until he caught up with the herd. The cattle were well up the steep arroyo toward Dead Man's Pass when he reached Killer.

"What was all the shootin' about back yonder?" Killer inquired.

Abel explained in grim, blunt words, then said, "You ramrod the herd over the summit, Killer. Spread them out in the lava breaks. I'm going back to town. Two of the rannies working for Dugger got away. There'll be the devil to pay when they tell their story. I've got to tell the people in town my true name and get their help in stopping any reprisal Dugger's bought sheriff might drum up."

CHAPTER FIFTEEN

Abel rode directly to the Curtis ranch, wanting to check on Denise and learn what he could of conditions in the town. He was no longer Cal Turner. He was Abel Fargo with his hate and purpose exposed. There had been enough tragedy at the stampede. If anything happened to Denise because of her allegiance to him, he could never forgive himself.

Things were happening much faster than he had planned. He had hoped to drive the herd off before its loss was discovered, but finding Fester Lomas and Cy Short there with the same idea had triggered the killing of three men. The two riders who had escaped would have reached town well ahead of him, and would have made their report to Max Dugger.

Max would claim a legitimate cause to raise a posse and hunt Abel and his men down. He had to prevent that. His subterfuge of buying into the bank would have no bearing on the outcome now. He had hoped to trap Dugger robbing the bank money, hiding it conveniently, and faking a holdup. There was no time for that now.

Abel reached the Curtis ranch without interference. It was near noon and the fact that Chris Curtis's horse was in the corral gave no warning that anything out of the ordinary was going on. Chris usually came home for the midday meal with Denise and his wife.

Abel left his horse in one of the stalls in the barn, but he didn't unsaddle him. He forked him some hay before going to the house. There was a peculiar quiet out in the yard. He saw Letha's buggy in front of the house with a drowsing Mexican in the driver's seat, his sombrero pulled over his eyes.

This disturbed him, but he decided Letha was about to take off to be with Alice at the birth of Tony's baby. He climbed the three steps to the back porch and let himself into the kitchen without knocking. The kitchen was deserted, but from the parlor he heard the sound of muffled sobs. A premonition gripped him like a vise.

Chris had been shot or beaten up because he had conspired to help Abel with his plans. A sickening wave of remorse overcame him as he walked into the darkened parlor.

Then Chris Curtis's voice rang out.

"Thank heaven you're here, Abel. All hell's broke loose."

Abel turned his eyes on Letha, lying on the couch and sobbing uncontrollably. "What is it, Chris? Is Letha shot?"

"Not Letha," Chris said.

"Den—Denise?"

"Not Denise. Tony's been a madman since you beat him up in the bar. He's been laid up at the Dugger house. Letha stayed there with Alice, not sure of what Tony might do. Then a tramp cowboy came from the Circle-F. He claimed he saw you an' Irma Dugger sneak outta the bank the other night. He said he trailed you and found you ridin' out to Tony's new house on the Circle-F. He said you were the same man who beat him up on Boot Hill, but he got away and hid out till he got proof that you were Abel Fargo, for whom there was a reward still standing."

"I wondered what became of that man." Abel hissed the words. "As heaven is my witness, Chris, I never dreamed it would end this way. Is Letha all right?"

"She ain't hurt physically, but she's in shock. Tony went loco when he heard what the cowboy had to say. He accused Alice of having you go out to the Circle-F to wait for her after the baby is born. He accused her of being in love with you. In his frenzy he shot the man who brought him the news of your presence and then he turned on Alice. He struck her blow after blow until she fell, hitting her head against the hearth. Letha fled in panic. She got Santos to drive her to the doctor where she told what had happened, and then she fainted. Santos brought her here."

Abel felt a cold, rigid armor of anger stop the trembling fury that enveloped him. His mind congealed into one clear resolve. He had to stop this maniacal drama that had resulted from his presence in Silverado. He had to destroy this new stream of hatred for which he was partly responsible.

"Where is Denise?" he said calmly.

"Her an' Paul took off for the Dugger house as soon as Letha got here. Their one thought was to save Alice. Alice is my own flesh and blood, Abel. She married Tony against my wishes, but she didn't marry him for love. She married him partly for our sake and partly for hate, determined to make him suffer for what he had done to the boy she had once loved."

"I've got to leave at once, Chris. I may not come back. You and Denise will know what to do if I am killed."

Abel bridled his horse and took off for town by the back trail. To ride up the main street might trigger a confrontation he wasn't ready for. He rode directly to Dugger's house, vaulted from the saddle at the gate, and walked to the porch in a dozen long strides. He flung the front door open, his gun ready for action.

Quiet greeted him. Denise was standing in the middle of the parlor, her face frozen with surprise at his sudden appearance. Before she could speak, he caught her in his arms and held her close.

"Thank heaven you're safe, Denny!" he exclaimed. "How's Alice?"

"I—I don't know," she whimpered. "How did you get here?"

"It's a long story. It can wait. Where's Paul?" Abel asked.

"He's gone for the sheriff."

"The sheriff? Why? Where's Tony?"

"I think he means to rob the bank and leave the country. He's like a man possessed. He means to kill you somehow, someway," she told him.

"Where's Irma and Mrs. Dugger?"

"Mrs. Dugger is hysterical. One of the servants put her to bed. Irma is down at the bank," Denise explained.

A feeling of dread was like a hand at Abel's throat, suffocating him. The memory of Irma washing and salving his bruised face, helping him secure the papers from the vault, came back to haunt him.

"Irma could be killed," he groaned. "She's no blood kin of Tony's. I've got to get down there before Tony harms her."

He left abruptly, his mind a froth of fury, fear, and contrition. No one must suffer because of him. If he had to die, so be it, but no one else must suffer, especially not Irma.

It was past closing time at the bank and he found the door locked. He banged on it, but there was no response. He had a sinking feeling that Irma had already been harmed. Without hesitation he smashed the frosted glass in the window beside the door. Unmindful of the jagged shards of glass, he crawled inside.

As he emerged in the room, he heard the voice—the deadly voice of Tony, filled with suppressed anger and determination.

"Don't be a fool, Pa! Grab those bags an' let's get goin'. You take care of the money. I'm goin' after Abel Fargo, who passed himself off as Cal Turner!"

"You're crazy, Tony! Kill me if you must, but you're

crazy—crazy!" Irma's voice was choked with emotion.

Abel's eyes became accustomed to the darkened interior. In one crimson flash of realization, he grasped the truth. Irma was slumped down on the floor. A red streak of blood smirched her white cheek. Her hand was up in a gesture of defense.

"Blast your dirty soul, Tony Dugger! If you must *kill,* kill me!" Abel cried.

Tony staggered like a man struck with a club. A look of utter disbelief crossed his face. Fate had sent his quarry to him.

"By heaven, Abel Fargo, you was dead once! This time it's goin'—"

"Hold it, Tony! We can handle it another way!" Max Dugger's voice came from the doorway of the vault room.

Abel kept his eyes on Tony, but he spoke to Max. "The way you once did, Max, when you murdered my family and set the house on fire? I nearly died and lost my memory when I escaped from the fire. But the Gypsies helped me. Now I've got my memory back. It came to me in a clear vision as I watched Gault's line shack burn. I saw you running away from the fire with the kerosene can in your hand!"

Abel kept his eyes on Tony. Max might kill him, but not before he killed Tony. He saw Tony's moment of indecision as death stalked between them. There was no turning back. One of them had to die. Tony had to make the first move. Abel's hand was away from his gun. Tony's shoulder twitched as he clawed his gun clear. Abel's hand moved like an invisible shadow.

The two guns roared as one. As he fired, Abel felt a hot flash of pain numb his right arm. His gun fell from his nerveless fingers. Tony was on his knees, his gun grasped in both hands. Abel kept his eyes on Tony as he braced himself for Max's bullet. Tony's finger tightened on the trigger. Abel made a desperate dive for his gun. The thought flashed through Abel's mind that this was it—the end of hate, killing, and deceit.

He heard other shots like distant echoes, but he kept his eyes on Tony. He snatched up his gun with his left hand. He turned to fire as Tony's gun roared. There was a scream. He saw a blurred figure between himself and Tony. The figure was that of Irma—she had taken the bullet meant for him!

He fired across Irma's prone body at Tony's weaving form. Once—twice—three times! The shots were a blur of sound. Blood spurted from Tony's chest and his mouth as he crashed back against Irma's desk. A bullet from a different direction struck Abel in the head. His last thought was that Max had again done his own dirty work; he had saved the reward money! Abel fell into a great pit of darkness—with no sound, no hate, no fury, and no pain.

When Abel came to, he saw Denise's face above him. Gentle hands were bathing the crease along his head. His wounded arm was swathed in bandages.

"Where—where am I?" he asked in a wheezy voice.

"You're on the floor in the bank where you fell, Abel," Denise told him.

He closed his eyes for a moment and then the stark reality of the past few moments stood out before him. He voiced the first thought that came into his mind.

"Where's Irma? Is—is she all right?"

Irma's own voice came from close beside him. "I'm all right, Abel, except for a bump on the head and a cut on my face."

Abel's voice was husky with emotion. "I—I thought you were dead, Irma—killed by a bullet meant for me."

"The bullet just grazed me. I knocked Tony's gun aside just as I fell, tripped by his bended knees. I lay there huddled down as your bullets screamed over me and killed Tony twice over."

"I heard other shots," Abel said.

"They were from the sheriff and Paul. Paul brought the sheriff, but instead of arresting Max and Tony, the sheriff joined them in trying to kill *you*. He creased your head. Then Paul killed the sheriff."

"Where's Paul now?" Abel asked.

"He's gone to Dugger's house to get the doctor. The doctor is treating Alice," Denise replied.

"How is Alice?"

"I don't know. I left the house and ran down here as soon as the doctor arrived. I told Doc there was trouble at the bank. I got here just after the shooting stopped."

Abel turned his head and looked up into Irma's beautiful face with its bridge of freckles and frame of red hair. "How's Max, Irma?"

"He's dead," Irma said without emotion.

"Who killed him?"

"Nobody. He died of a heart attack in all the excitement. He meant to kill you, Abel. I would have killed him myself to save you," Irma confessed.

"You've already done more than I can repay, Irma.

I came here seeking justice and I've created havoc," Abel lamented.

Just then the doctor and Paul arrived.

"What kind of a mess have we got here?" the doctor inquired.

"It's under control, Doc," Irma said, "except for removing the bodies."

"How's Alice making out?" Abel inquired.

"She's dead."

"Good heaven!" Abel said.

"The baby—how's the baby?" Denise asked, sobbing quietly.

"The baby died with her," the doctor said without emotion. "Maybe Tony can answer to them when he passes them on his road to the devil."

"It's all got to mean something—all this pain and death—something more than just revenge for what was done to my family years ago. I owe you the rest of my life, Denise," Abel said in a halting voice.

"You don't owe me anything, Abel. Quit belittling yourself. All you did was bring the festering boil to a head in Silverado. The ranchers in the valley can breathe freely again now. You've silenced the guns of tranquility and the killers who skulked behind them. If you're thinking about marrying me, forget it. There'd be a shadow between us, the shadow of Emil. In a corner of my mind I'd still wonder which twin you were, Abel or Emil. If you owe anybody your life it's Irma. She put her own life on the line by helping you expose Max, her foster father. When Paul said he was going to marry me, he meant it, and I'm not averse to the idea," Denise said, clinging to Paul's arm. "I'm deeply sad about Alice and the baby," she added, "but Alice made her own decision. Now at least her torment is over."

A moment of silence followed Denise's sobering words. Abel looked up at Irma, and drew her toward him.

"You heard what the girl said, freckles?" There was a twinkle in his eye, and a new ring to his voice.

"I'll freckle you after we're married. You can call me honey. You can call me dear. You can call me wifey. But not freckles. It would sound funny to our kids. We're partners already—in the bank, that is. When you say I do, I'll sign my share over to you. Mother won't mind just so she's taken care of in the manner to which she's become accustomed."

Abel held her face and kissed her. "We've got a ranch, too, you know."

"I'll be the best little ranch wife you ever saw. I'll cook, slop the hogs, take care of the kids, and help with the roundup. I'll get dried out and wrinkled and ornery," Irma warned him.

"You'll always be young and beautiful in my heart, honey," Abel said, holding her close beside him and smothering her with kisses.